I0782084

“The Christmas Cabin”
edited by Shannon Maddox

“Interlude,” “A Christmas Robbery,” and “The Road to Christmas”
edited by Dani J. Caile

WRITE CROWD PUBLISHING

The Christmas Cabin

2. Patrick Lemarr

For the *Author* of every story.

"And that, of course, is the message of Christmas. We are never alone. Not when the night is darkest, the wind coldest, the world seemingly most indifferent..."

Taylor Caldwell

Table of Contents

THE CHRISTMAS CABIN

The *old farm road* leading away from the interstate deep into the Tennessee hills was carpeted in snow and ice. All sanding and salting efforts had been relegated to the highways, which meant locals in need of traversing the snowy back roads would have to do so at their own risk.

In her all-wheel-drive rental car, Samantha Cobb

had assumed the weather wouldn't be a factor. But, as her vehicle lost traction time and time again along the one lane dirt road leading to her parents' cabin, she began to wonder if she would have to temporarily abandon her plans and call for roadside assistance.

The smarmy radio DJ suggested the wintry downpour could continue for the next three days.

"That's fine," she thought. "Christmas Eve is tomorrow. It can snow all it damn well pleases."

The last half a mile to the cabin was mostly uphill and her rental fought for every inch it climbed. Midway up a particularly steep stretch, she lost traction and slid backward a few yards before slowing to a stop. The back wheels refused to do anything but spin in place.

"Oh, come on," she whispered. "I can practically see the cabin from here. Just a little further."

Unmoved by her encouragement, the car refused to grip the road.

She got out of the vehicle and looked for anything she could put under the tires to provide a bit of traction. When she found nothing alongside the road, she rifled through the contents of her baggage and stuffed an old college sweatshirt as far under one of the tires as she could manage. Under the other, she wedged a paperback copy of *Borrowed and Blue* she was certain she'd never read again. It wasn't much, but it was what she had to work with, so she climbed back in the driver's seat and tried to get the car moving again.

She could feel the wheels spinning in the back, even as the front wheels struggled to hold onto their purchase.

"Just a little more," she said through clenched teeth.

She pressed harder on the gas and felt the car straining to surge forward. Then, pedal to the metal, she began to rock the vehicle, hoping to free it from the rut it was in. Her plan worked all too well. The rental shot out of its furrow and spun wildly on the ice, turning her car back downhill where it began to slide once more.

Samantha had no control.

In her effort to free the tires, she hadn't noticed the windshield fogging up which, along with the constant drift of snow, afforded her near zero visibility. As the car skated down the hill, she found she couldn't see the road ahead.

But something stood out amid the stark white of the snow-blanketed countryside. She squinted and tried to focus, worried it was a fence post or the remnants of a tree. Either would mean she had already left the relative safety of the road. By the time she recognized the shape as a man, however, it was too late to avoid him.

Before she could even honk, the man dove out of her way.

It was then the car slid sideways and rolled—with

a screech of twisted metal and broken glass—side over side until it wound its way off the road and lodged itself upside down against an old tree. She lost consciousness, battered by the airbags that saved her life.

Samantha awoke to a familiar scent. Her head felt the wrong size, as though it had been used as the puck in a frenzied game of hockey. As she forced her eyes open, she found a stranger smiling down at her.

"Hey there," he said, brushing his shaggy brown hair out of his eyes. "Best not to try and move just yet. You might have a concussion."

To her eyes, he seemed not much older than a college freshman in his worn blue jeans and plain black t-shirt. Behind his eyes, however, was a wisdom that belied his youth…an otherworldly depth that gave her pause.

"W-Where am I?"

"Not far from where your car went off the road," he said. "I assumed this was your place. You had the key on your keychain…which I discovered after a bit of trial and error."

"My rental car—"

"Is resting upside down against a tree about three-quarters of a mile down the hill. There was fuel leaking into the snow, so I risked moving you. I tried to get you an ambulance, but the storm seems to have messed with cell phone reception up here. This was the only shelter in sight. I hope you don't mind."

"Is that coffee I smell?"

He smiled at her again.

She thought his face was as kind as it was handsome.

"It is. I managed to salvage some of the supplies in your trunk," he said. "You lost a couple of bottles of wine, I'm afraid. And your sandwich bread got a bit smushed. But most everything else survived. Including us."

"I almost hit you!" she suddenly remembered.

"I'm not offended. You had no control of your car at the time."

"Who are you?"

"My name's Dylan Drake," he said. "After I found the water valve and turned it on, I brewed some coffee hoping to warm myself up a little, though the fire I lit in the hearth is doing the better job of it. There's plenty left. Would you like a cup?"

She shook her head not realizing how badly such a

simple movement would hurt.

"How did we get up here?"

"I threw you over my shoulder and carried you," he admitted. "It was a bit awkward and slow-going, but we made it. And I only had to eat a few pounds of snow to get it done."

"You saved me," she said.

"Nonsense. I just happened to be in the right place at the wrong time. Or maybe the wrong place at the right time. Whichever way you'd care to look at it, I suppose. How long have you had this place?"

"I inherited it. It belonged to my parents. They called it their Christmas cabin."

"Christmas cabin? Is that a Tennessee thing I don't know about?"

"No. It's just what my parents called it. Nearly every year these hills get snow between Christmas and New Year, so they'd drag us up here for the holidays. No phone. No TV. Just family. Mom would do all the cooking, and Papa would entertain us with his concertina."

Seeing the perplexed look on the stranger's face, she chuckled.

"A concertina is like a tiny accordion. My father could play anything on it."

"Sounds nice."

"It was."

"Us?"

"Pardon?"

"You said 'they'd drag *us* up here.' You have siblings?"

"I did have. A sister. Mikhela."

"That's a pretty name."

"We called her Mike," Samantha said, ignoring the image of her sister which flashed through her mind. "She could sing like a bird, our Mikhela. Made grown men cry when she'd sing those sad country songs she loved so much."

"Older or younger?"

"She was younger than me by a couple of years. She was killed in a bus crash a few years ago."

"I'm so sorry."

The young man's eyes held such empathy Samantha found it uncomfortable to meet his gaze.

"I hate to ask," she said, "but could you help me get to the bathroom, Dylan? I'm feeling awfully woozy, and I'd rather not do any more damage to myself just yet."

"Of course," he said, offering her a hand. "And, if I may, you might want to give yourself a once-over while you're in there. I cleaned a small cut on your forehead, but your car took quite a tumble. You could be injured in places I couldn't see."

"Gentlemanly of you not to have a look," she said,

leaning on him. "I appreciate it."

"Decency doesn't require thanks," he said. "I felt your arms and legs briefly enough to make sure nothing major was broken, but I'd be surprised if you don't have bruises. Swelling, though, could mean trouble. If you find any, let me know."

"You a doctor, Dylan?"

"I don't even play one on TV," he replied, slowly walking her down the short hallway to the cabin's only bathroom. "I *do*, however, have a bit of experience with broken bones."

"I'll check for bruises," she assured. "But, even if I find swelling or worse, not much can be done without a cell phone signal."

"I could hike back down if I needed to," he said. "Get some help and bring it back."

"Likely not necessary but thank you."

His eyes narrowed, searching hers.

"You don't know if it's necessary or not, ma'am. You haven't checked."

"Okay, Doc. I'll let you know."

She took a deep breath, her mind awash in a sea of thoughts. None of them were helped by the concussion. After Dylan helped her steady herself at the small sink, he left, and Samantha closed the door behind him.

"Please be careful," the young man admonished

through the door. "And, if you feel dizzy and need help getting back, just say the word."

Samantha examined her face in the small oval mirror her mother had hung above the small sink long ago. It had been one of Mabel Cobb's infamous garage sale finds she had lovingly restored and given a new life. The mirror was but one of dozens of such items in the Christmas cabin.

Samantha located the cut Dylan had mentioned—though he had done a fine job of patching it—along with a few bruised places that would likely look much worse within a few days.

She carefully pulled her gray wool sweater over her head and hung it from the towel hook on the back of the door. She found no other cuts or bruises above her waist. She removed her jeans and checked her legs. Nothing broken. Nothing scarred. There was, however, a tender spot on her left hip that might eventually develop a bruise.

'Not that I'll give it the time,' she thought.

Standing there in nothing but her underwear, she looked at the face staring back at her. It looked old to her eyes, and weary—like the women photographed in the Dust Bowl era when life was so hard a woman could age a decade within just a few desperate weeks.

After emptying her bladder, she splashed some cold

water on her face and steeled herself for dealing with the handsome young man. As kind as he had been, she needed him gone. She mentally prepared the lies she would tell him as she dressed.

When Samantha returned to the main room of the tiny cabin, she found Dylan tending the fire. Next to him sat his unfinished mug of coffee in her father's favorite Tennessee Titans mug.

"Bruise free for the most part," she told him. "Though I'm guessing a few might be delayed by a day or two."

"And your head?"

"Just as messy as always," she said, circling her index finger near her temple, "but less dizzy than before."

She sat on the old second-hand couch her mother had purchased for the place. It was overstuffed and worn and felt good to her tired bones. Draped across the back of the couch was an afghan her mother and father had received as a wedding gift from a cousin who passed away shortly before Samantha was born. It was hopelessly outdated, but her mother had refused to part with it.

The stranger seemed so comfortable sipping his coffee and tending the fire she could almost imagine the cabin was actually his and she was the interloper.

"Do you live around here, Dylan? Ober, maybe, or somewhere else in the mountains?"

"No, ma'am. I was born in New York, but I grew up mainly in the suburbs of Chicago. I'm afraid a city boy like me wouldn't know much about living in the mountains."

"No need to call me ma'am. My name is Samantha. My family and friends call me Sam. Considering all you've done, you fall into the latter category."

"I appreciate it, Sam, but I didn't really do much. You'd have crawled out of the wreckage without me. I'm just glad you didn't have to. It might have taken a while."

"There's not much down this road except this little Christmas cabin. What brings you out here?"

"I've often heard about how beautiful a Tennessee Christmas can be, so I decided to see for myself," he said after a sip of his coffee. "I made the mistake of going for a walk in the snow. I didn't really have a destination in mind…but the weather makes it hard to tell up from down."

"Are you in town for the holidays? Visiting family and such?"

"No, ma'a…I mean, Sam. I don't have any family in this part of the country. My mom still lives in the Chicago area. I'll be seeing her on Christmas Day, same as always. Assuming the weather breaks and I can get down the mountain, of course."

"And your father?"

He looked down at the floor between them before meeting her gaze.

"My dad passed away before I was born."

Samantha nodded but said nothing.

"The weather seems to be determined," Dylan said, peeking past the colorful curtains to the still-falling snow. "I'll bet what's left of your rental will be barely visible in another hour. Speaking of which, I sure hope you paid for the damage waiver."

"I did. Did you say you couldn't get a cell signal?"

"Yes, ma'am," he said, fishing her phone from his pocket. "Your phone survived without a scratch, but I couldn't get signal enough for 911."

Samantha unlocked her phone and checked. It was just as Dylan said. Zero bars.

"Did you try *your* phone?"

"I don't carry one," Dylan replied.

"Your job doesn't require you to carry one?" Before he could answer, she added, "Or are you a student?"

"I suppose I'm taking a bit of a gap year. Been doing some editing work."

"Editing?"

"Yes, ma'am."

Samantha gave him a stern look.

"Sorry. *Sam.*"

"What exactly do you edit?"

"Whatever stories my employer asks me to, really. He's quite prolific, so there's always work to be done. What about you, Sam? What do you do?"

Samantha pulled her feet onto the couch and rested her sore head on the overstuffed armrest.

"I'm a market analyst. I work for several large firms to figure out how to boost their sales each quarter and worm their way into new markets when good opportunities arise. Basically, I help rich people get richer."

"Someone's got to do it I suppose," Dylan replied. "I'll bet the pay is nice."

"Oh, sure. If you don't mind working 60-hour weeks and flying all over the map on a moment's notice."

"It must make coming home for Christmas more exciting, though. To leave the hustle and bustle behind for a few days and spend Christmas with the people you love."

Samantha closed her eyes and took a deep breath. The cabin smelled the same as it always did: the burning hickory in the fireplace mixed with the aroma of freshly brewed coffee. It sounded the same, as well. The stillness of the air punctuated by the sound of crackling embers. She could almost imagine nothing had changed.

"Mike and Sam, huh?" Dylan asked.

Startled out of her own thoughts, Samantha only managed, "What?"

"You and your sister. Sam and Mike. Someone in the family wanted boys, I take it?"

"Less that and more that we were both tomboys," Samantha said, smiling and shaking her head. "Sal and Mabel Cobb's double trouble. We were always climbing trees, hopping fences, and trying things anyone with half a brain wouldn't dare."

The smile left her face as swiftly as it had arrived.

Dylan remained silent for a moment before continuing.

"I'm sorry if I overstepped. Those sound like sweet memories."

"No. You're…fine."

"Can I fix you something to eat? Our supplies may be limited to what survived your crash, but remarkably nine of your dozen eggs survived. I can fry up some bacon to go with them if you like."

"Help yourself," she said, smiling despite her mood. It wasn't often she saw such kindness in strangers. She almost hated having to run him off. "None for me, though. I think I'll just rest."

"I'm not hungry, so I'll wait until you feel like eating. But, Sam, I'm not sure it's safe for you to nap. You were unconscious for a good half-hour and I'm pretty sure a concussion requires me to keep you awake."

"You can try, Dylan, but I've hardly slept the last

few nights. I was exhausted long before the airbag collided with my face. Besides, I'm pretty sure that bit of medical advice went away with leeches and blood-letting."

"They actually still use leeches to improve blood flow to tissue," Dylan said, taking the afghan from the back of the sofa and tucking it in around Samantha. "Let's not dismiss good medical advice just because it's old-fashioned."

She focused on his handsome face and smiled.

"You can wake me up every hour if it makes you feel better, Hero. But I might bite you. I'm pretty feral when I'm overly tired."

Dylan laughed.

She thought he had a good laugh.

"I'll take my chances if it will keep you safe, Sam. And, once you've had some rest, you need to eat. We may have to dig our way out of here in the morning."

Samantha nodded though she had no intention of leaving the cabin alive.

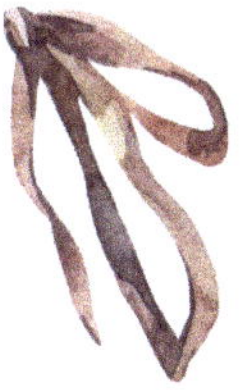

In her dreams, Samantha saw the Christmas cabin as it had been when she was a child. Back then, it hadn't seemed small or musty but larger than life and packed to the rafters with the sort of magic only the holiday season could hold for young children.

Her mother was there working on the Christmas tree, hanging strands of popcorn she had carefully threaded herself. Tradition dictated the whole family would pick out the tree together and drive to the cabin with it tied down to the luggage rack of her father's rusted out Bronco. Her father, Sal, would play his concertina in his favorite chair while Mike, clad in her Christmas pajamas—Mama bought them each a new pair every year—danced joyfully to his jaunty version of "O Christmas Tree", singing along breathlessly.

Sam could almost smell the ham roasting in the oven, its heavenly scent mingling with the spiced apple cider Mama kept warm on the stove.

Unbidden, reality began to encroach on her dream. A mangled bus. A stark hospital room. Papa's empty chair. Those flashes abandoned her to a cabin now devoid of life. The oven and hearth sat cold. An orb-weaver spider built its home in the corner where a Christmas tree once stood. The only scent detectable in the air was the stale hint of mildew from the cabin sitting empty too long. Once a place of great joy and fond memories, it had become like a tomb.

Then the cabin itself was gone entirely. Samantha stood alone in the cemetery just a few miles down the highway. Alongside the three headstones she had helped pick out, a fresh grave had been dug as a grim invitation.

Samantha awoke to Dylan's friendly face shrouded with concern as he jostled her back into the world of the living.

"Was I snoring?"

"No," he said, "but you've been asleep for several hours and I thought you should eat."

Samantha used her left hand to shield her eyes from the nearly blinding sunlight streaming in through the curtains.

"What time is it?"

"About 10am. Merry Christmas Eve. How are you feeling?"

"Better now," she said, sitting upright on the couch. "Sore but alert. Did you sleep?"

"A bit. I went out for a few minutes after you dozed off to gather more firewood from the stack near the fence. After I made sure the fire would last the night, I dozed a bit in the big chair in the corner."

"It was my dad's favorite."

"I can see why. I woke up a few hours ago and checked outside. Snow is still coming down. I can't see much past the fence line. I decided some coffee and breakfast might be just what the non-doctor ordered."

"It smells good," she admitted.

"Sit tight. I'll fix you a plate."

True to his word, Dylan brought her a plate loaded with scrambled eggs, thick-cut bacon, and roasted red potatoes. Samantha wolfed it down like she hadn't eaten in weeks.

"You're a good cook, Dylan."

"My mom is a good cook," he corrected. "I'm just good at mimicking what I've seen her do a million times. I learn from watching."

"Did you learn anything from watching me sleep?"

She couldn't decide if she was annoyed by Dylan interfering with her plans or touched by his compassion and kindness.

"After about the 3rd time I woke you—"

"I don't remember you waking me."

"I did. A few times. About the 3rd, I realized you were doing alright, so I just let you sleep."

Sam took a sip of her coffee and then stretched her legs.

"Any luck with the cell?"

"I haven't tried," he admitted. "It was in your pocket."

She smiled sheepishly and dug it out to check for a signal.

"Nada. I guess we've no choice but to wait it out."

"Could be worse. We could be stranded all alone. I, for one, appreciate the company."

"Maybe we'll get a signal later in the day," she said. "Then we can call an Uber or something and get you home."

"Anxious to be rid of me?"

The compassion she found behind his hazel eyes made her want to tell him the truth. But she didn't.

"Of course not. I just don't want your mom to worry about you."

"While you were sleeping, I found the water heater and lit the pilot. There should be enough hot water for a shower by now. Might help loosen up any of the tension in your muscles caused by the crash."

Her eyes narrowed.

"You aren't secretly a masseur, too, are you, Dylan?"

She was flirting with him. She knew she shouldn't, especially given her plans, but she couldn't help herself. She had never met anyone quite like him.

"No, ma'am. I just figured a hot shower and some

clean clothes might make you feel better."

"And what will you do while I'm showering?"

"Wash the breakfast dishes."

"You're quite the catch, if you don't mind me saying so."

"I don't think nearly killing me with your car equals catching me," he said. "I'm just trying to earn my keep. You *are* sheltering me from a sizeable storm, after all."

She left him there and showered, letting the hot water soothe the aches and pains of her accident. The strong, perfume-heavy soap she had found under the sink awakened her senses as her residual tiredness slipped away and washed down the drain with the suds.

Sam wrapped a towel around herself and realized she hadn't asked Dylan where he had put her things.

'Oh, damn,' she thought, turning to check herself out in the mirror. 'Hot guy in the next room and me in just a towel. I suppose there are worse ways to thank him for his kindness.'

She walked out of the bathroom and straight to the kitchen where she found Dylan seasoning her mother's favorite cast iron skillet with the flaxseed oil she kept on hand for that purpose.

"Dylan, I have a question for you."

He turned to answer and then, seeing her clad in only her towel, averted his eyes back to the cast iron.

The fact that he blushed made him even more attractive to her.

"Yes, ma'am?"

"Stop it. My name is Sam. Calling me 'ma'am' makes me feel positively ancient. I don't *look* ancient, do I, Dylan?"

Edging 25, Samantha had always taken great pains to retain her slender figure. She was no waif. She was a Tennessee tomboy. But she filled out her towel in all the right ways and had little doubt any young man would appreciate the view.

"No offense, Sam," Dylan replied without looking up, "but I'm not going to offer an appraisal while you're standing there nearly naked."

"Gosh, I didn't mean to embarrass you. I wasn't sure where you'd put my bag is all."

"As I'm certain you know, this cabin just has one bedroom, so I put your luggage in there. I only left you on the couch last night so I could keep an eye on you."

She sauntered closer until her toes were nearly touching his Converse sneakers.

"But you won't keep an eye on me now? Even if I'd really like you to?"

Dylan looked up from the cast iron to meet her gaze. Suddenly Samantha felt like the intimidated one, though she fought the urge to look away.

"You're a beautiful woman, Sam. But what you need from me, you'll never get this way. I want to help you, but this—you coming onto me—is a lie. Whether you're trying to tell it to yourself or to me, I won't hazard to guess."

The resolve she found in his eyes intrigued her.

"What if I want you to kiss me? To make me feel alive?"

"I won't kiss you. I'm sorry, but I won't."

"Am I so ugly?"

"Far from it."

"Too old?"

"No, Sam."

"Then what? Why can't we take warmth where we find it?"

"Go put on some clothes. If you still want to know why I won't kiss you, you can ask me then."

She leaned in closer, but Dylan remained resolute, refusing to close the distance.

"I'm asking you now."

The young man's eyes never changed. He was not cowed by her forwardness nor angered by her disregarding his wishes. If he thought any less of her for her efforts at seducing him, it didn't sour the compassion he wore as easily as his black t-shirt.

"Okay, then. You want to know, so I'll tell you. We'll cut through the pretense. First, Sam, my heart—and all the rest of me—belongs to someone else. Or it will, whenever I can commit to it. Second, I don't believe seeking solace in a random sexual encounter can provide you with the sort of 'alive' feeling you seem to be aching for. You're mistaking a spiritual and emotional need for physical desire. It's cheap and shallow and its thrill wouldn't satisfy you for long. Third, and most importantly, I know you plan to kill yourself tomorrow, and a kiss with no potential seems especially hollow to me…no matter how lovely the potential partner."

She backed away from him, gripping the towel where it was secured at her breasts.

"Who *are* you?"

"Dylan Drake," he replied, turning back to continue seasoning the skillet. "You almost ran me over with your car, remember? And I dragged you all the way up the hill to make sure you were okay. If you think I did all those things just to watch you kill yourself, you've got another thing coming."

"H-How do you—?"

"Know what you've been planning? It's why I'm here, Sam. I'm an editor, remember? It's my job to fix the bad parts of a story. The parts that don't work. And killing yourself doesn't work. Not for the Author of your story. He's got so many great things planned for you but, if you check out now, you'll never get to them."

"Get out!"

"Sam, I can't leave. Not yet. Like it or not, you and I are stuck together through Christmas."

"This is my cabin," she said, "and I want you out. Now! Whoever you are, I don't want you here!"

"I know. It makes it inconvenient to end your own life when you have an audience watching. I'm an unpleasant reminder that people still care about you. That there's more to life than your sorrow."

She stormed out of the room and into what had once been her parent's bedroom. She hoped the strange young man would be gone by the time she stopped sobbing and dressed.

Samantha wasn't sure what to say when she exited the bedroom to find Dylan tending the fire once again. Though she had hoped he would leave, she hadn't really expected it. He was too kind to abandon her to her plans. But she had questions.

"How did you know?"

As she sat on the couch, he remained on the floor

near the hearth.

"About your decision?"

"Yes."

"Like I said, Sam. I'm an editor. Your story, like all others, is yours to navigate as you please. Like any good story, though, it has an Author who cares for His creations. He saw you steering toward an end you were never meant for, and He sent me to intervene."

"You're saying God sent you?"

"The Author is known by different names in different places. I suppose you can call Him whatever you wish. I know Him simply as the Author."

"So, you're what, an angel?"

"Oh, no ma'am. Angels dress much nicer than I do. They're a touch scary too, come to think about it. Not mean or anything, just...they don't much look like us unless they have a reason to."

"First, stop calling me 'ma'am', Dylan. It makes me want to punch you. Second, I don't buy it. God or… the Author or whatever you call Him clearly doesn't care about people or we wouldn't—"

"Die? Yes! Sam, people die. We're finite and fragile. We have a shelf life. An expiration date. It's just how it is."

"Why?"

"Because things are broken, and we add to the brokenness every day. The Author is still at work, though. Editing here. Mending a shattered heart there. Eventually it will all be made right again…no matter how much we try to get in His way."

"I don't believe in that stuff, Dylan. I don't believe you're an angel. I don't believe you're the ghost of Christmas Present or *any* of it. You're just a guy who's getting on my last damn nerve."

"Because I care about you?"

"Care? You don't even know me, Dylan!"

"Sure, I do. I've read through your life, Sam. It all started with the love story of Sal and Mabel Cobb. I came to care about them. And then you. And then Mike."

He paused a moment and stretched.

"Did you know it took your parents nearly five years of trying to finally have a child? They had given up on the notion, truth be told. Thought it just wasn't in the cards. It didn't stop them from praying for it, though, or from hoping in those deep-down places you can't really give voice to. And then you came, followed closely by your sister. Sam and Mike…'the Tennessee Terrors' as your dad used to say. The two of you broke three highchairs before Mike was old enough to sit in a big chair."

"How do you know those things?"

"Like I said, Sam. I've read your story. It's how I know you regret not coming to this cabin in 2017. None of you knew it would be the last family Christmas before Mike's death. The following year there was no celebration. You and your dad spent the holidays at your mom's bedside at Vanderbilt. Mabel held on into the new year, but you and Sal both knew it was the end. She had grown so weak so fast."

"Stop it."

"Sal had been wrapped up in taking care of your mom. He had neglected his own health. Leaving you alone wasn't his intention. His heart was just under too much strain."

"I don't…I can't take any more."

"We always live our lives as though we have all the time in the world, don't we? But we don't. Which is why, even when we see it coming like you did with your mom, it always seems sudden when we lose someone. A part of us was holding onto the notion that we'd say the things we needed to say the next time we saw them. Or we'd have another opportunity for a hug. We always assume there will be Christmases to come, but we don't always get another chance at those moments."

"Please, Dylan! Please, just…stop!"

"I'm not being cruel, Sam. I'm being honest. Your running full tilt away from reality is what led you to concoct this stupid plan."

"I don't want to be here without them. There's

nothing left for me."

"Nothing? Are you so sure?"

Samantha ground her teeth and sniffed back her emotions. Her eyes darted around the cabin and then back to the young man.

To Dylan, she seemed less like a wounded young woman than a caged animal, frightened and desperate.

"I'm not here to stop you," he said. "Not physically, anyway. If you choose to go through with things, you can. But I hope to convince you otherwise."

"Why? Because it's your job?"

"Yes. But also…well, I like you, Sam. Truly. When I research the people I'm sent to help, it's usually just me reading the basics so I can develop the right approach and do the most good. But the more I read of your story the more I felt like I knew you."

"You don't."

"I said I felt like it. I remember reading about Sal building the treehouse you and Mike wanted for your backyard. The one with the rope and pulley."

"For lifting all our toys up there," Samantha remembered.

"He had been laid off that spring. I don't know if he ever told you. Lumber prices were high and he…well, he scavenged all he could from local job sites. He had promised his girls a treehouse and they were getting one come hell or high water. He did a lot of odd jobs to keep food on the table…to keep the misery of the world from finding its way into his family."

"He made everything seem right as rain."

"So did your mom. Reading about Mabel, she reminded me of my own mom. I don't get to see her often these days. I meant what I said, though. I hope to spend Christmas with her, once I know my work here is done."

Samantha sat up straight and examined the young man's eyes.

"You're really just a regular guy?"

"Flesh and blood. No different than you."

"If I believed you—and I'm not saying I do—isn't interfering in other people's lives a dangerous job for… essentially a kid?"

"Was I a kid when you were throwing yourself at me in the kitchen?"

"Fair, but still a low blow, Dylan."

"I'm nearly twenty if I remember correctly. Time gets confusing when you bounce around as much as I do. I was in space a few weeks ago…although, from your perspective, it would be in the distant future."

"You weren't in space. Or the future."

Dylan crossed his heart and raised his right hand.

"People can't do those things," she insisted.

"This people can."

"So, you're just some rando dude that wanders from place-to-place—throughout time, no less—fixing people's lives?"

"That's…a bit of an oversimplification. Every life is a story. And every story is a life. Somewhere. In one reality or another. I step into a tale whenever hope is in short supply or helplessness has taken root. I go wherever I'm needed."

"Every story is a life. Do you hear yourself? That's word salad! What does that even mean?"

"It means every bit of fiction you've read is reality somewhere else. And your story, Sam, could be fiction for readers elsewhere."

She rolled her eyes and shook her head.

"Hogwarts, Narnia, and Derry, Maine are all, what? Real places in some other universe?"

"Other branches of reality. Yes."

"You're ridiculous."

"I am. But I'm also telling you the truth."

"Okay, then. Thrill me. What else have you seen? What crazy places have you been?"

He studied her eyes for a moment and then sighed.

"It's hard to know where to start, really. I've been at this a lot longer than my age would suggest. I don't grow older when I'm outside the context of my own narrative."

"Sure. Of course," she said flatly. "As my favorite philosopher once said: 'Here we are now, entertain us.'"

"Some of the highlights, then. 15th century Spain. Victorian London. Fought vampires there. Well, my mentor did most of the fighting. I was young back then. Maybe too young."

He scratched absentmindedly at his chin as he thought.

"I got shot once trying to save a guy mixed up with the wrong people. Thankfully, I had a wizard around to heal me up as good as new. Not too long ago, I stopped a maniacal wannabe god from destroying the people and the town he loved. That was cool. And I met Sherlock Holmes. He was shorter than I thought he'd be."

Samantha crossed her arms.

"Prove it."

Dylan's lip curled with the barest hint of a smile.

"I could."

"But?"

"I won't."

"That's what I thought."

"No. You think I won't because I *can't*. You think I'm full of it. Which is fine. I get it. But it's all true and I could prove it."

"Then why won't you?"

"Because I've already told you things I couldn't possibly know, Sam. If what I know about your family and their history wasn't enough to convince you, why would I jump through your hoops now? You'd only find another reason to dismiss me."

"Why would I do that?"

"Because you simply don't want to believe."

"Should I? I'll admit you've got a few stunning parlor tricks."

"Well, that's just…mean."

"But I don't even know if any of what you told me is true. Maybe my folks had me on their first attempt."

"They didn't."

"Says you."

Dylan laughed.

"I knew you were a mess when I came here, Sam. A smart, stubborn, charming, irritating, beautiful mess."

"Beautiful? If you really thought so, you'd have kissed me."

"Not everything is *for* you, Sam. Not everything is about you. Such twisted thinking is what led you here, where you're dangerously close to throwing away the Author's greatest gift."

"Gift." Samantha scoffed.

"You don't think so? You'd rather have never known them?"

"What?"

"Your family. That you had them at all was grace, Sam. Do you have any idea how many people—no, let's narrow it to just children—how many children would love to have even half the stability, love, and devotion you had growing up? Some kids go through life never knowing their fathers. Some are raised by people so wrapped up in their own damage or addictions they abuse and torment the very souls they should protect. But you, Sam, had two parents who loved each other even more than they loved you and Mike. They sowed more laughter, hope, love, and compassion into you than many will ever experience in an entire lifetime. And, sure, I understand you would have rather had them around longer, but…you had them. They were all yours. And that didn't have to happen. It wasn't owed to you. It was given."

"Then what should I do with all this pain, Dylan? Suck it up? Is that the heavenly wisdom you're offering me? Just suck up the aching hole I feel in the center of my life every time I want to call my mom and ask her to send me the recipe for her Christmas cookies? Every time I want to ask my dad if the mechanic is trying to rip me off? Every time I hear someone on the radio with half the talent Mike had?"

"I would never tell you to just suck it up. I told you earlier…my dad died before I was born. I had a million moments growing up when I wished I could just ask him how to survive the nonsense of life. I fell into this impossible job when I was young, Sam. Too young to bear so much responsibility. But I had a mentor who tried to prepare me for this crazy life I live, and I've made some friends along the way. I made it. I'm a real, *whole* person with no small amount of joy and love in my life. But I still miss what I never had. I feel an empty spot, too."

"I'm sorry, Dylan. I don't really know what to believe about you, but…I believe you miss your dad. Or, at the very least, the idea of him."

"I go from place to place doing my level best to help people. And sometimes, my work requires me to spend an inordinate amount of time in one spot. I come to care about the people I serve."

He paused and took a deep breath. After letting it out slowly, he continued.

"I come to love them…and be loved by them. And then, I leave. And it hurts, Sam. Every time. I could stop. I could quit this gig and go home. Take a few classes or learn a trade. I could leave this crazy draining work of loving and helping people behind, but I don't. You know why?"

Samantha shook her head.

"Because hurting is part of loving. Even back home, settled into a normal life, I would lose people. I'd love them and sooner or later they would move or eventually…die. And I would still hurt."

"Then why bother?"

"Because the hurt is just a moment in the vast scheme of things, Sam. The memories, the laughter, and the joy…it all gets rooted down deep inside me when I love and serve people well. It sustains me. It's so much stronger and lasts so much longer than the pain of loss. But right now, you've got your eyes set only on sorrow. You're ignoring the grace of having loved them. Of being loved by them. Of time spent. Of memories made which you'll cherish forever. Of tears shed with them when your heart broke for them or theirs broke for you. You're a woman rich beyond the telling with what really matters. And you're too busy trying to hide from your sorrow to let the grace of what you had rescue you."

"I miss them, Dylan. I'm not sure I can ever get past it. You should've just let me die out there on the road."

"You were never going to die in that crash, Sam. You have a mild concussion and a few bruises…the same injuries you'd have if I hadn't shown up. If death is what you really want—and I don't believe it is—you'll have to do the deed yourself."

"You think I won't?"

"I know part of you thinks it would be the easiest solution. But there's another part of you—a bigger part,

I think—not ready to check out. Even without the food you lost in the crash, you packed enough to extend past Christmas in case you changed your mind. You also admitted you paid for the damage waiver on your rental. Those don't seem like things you'd bother with if you thought you wouldn't live past the weekend."

"You think it's some kind of proof that I won't go through with it?"

"I don't know, Sam. I hope you won't. But, like everyone else in this story, you've got the free will to do whatever you'd like. Even something selfish."

"Selfish?"

She sat up straight on the couch, glaring at him.

"You think I'm selfish?"

"Yes. Short-sighted, too."

"Then explain to me, Clarence, why I'm selfish."

"And short-sighted," Dylan reminded. He rose from his spot by the fire and sat next to her on the couch. "Checking out suggests your story is all about you. But your parents had their own story and so did Mike. You got to be a part of those stories, sure, but they weren't just players in the movie of your life, you know. They understood something seemingly lost on you; your life isn't about you. You are part of a tapestry woven from strands as diverse and complex as you can imagine. You have a part to play, Sam, but you aren't the center of the universe. Not even your own."

"Your brilliant scheme is to *kumbaya* me into believing I have some big part to play in someone else's story?"

"You might."

"I might not. I might be completely unimportant."

"I've been all over creation, Sam. To times and worlds that would absolutely blow your mind. I've fought dragons, traveled at light speed, been trapped in a loop of time, and met a future version of me. And not once, in several lifetimes worth of service, have I ever met a man, woman, or child who wasn't important."

He reached across the distance between them and took her hand. It was a simple gesture of compassion.

"You once understood your life wasn't your own. You gave yourself fully to the people you loved. And maybe you lost your ability to love with abandon along the way. But you remember it, Sam. How good life could feel when career and status wasn't your driving aim. When you measured your success in laughter and time invested in the people you love."

"And who should I invest in now? Hmm? They're all gone, Dylan! They left me alone! Last year, I sat in front of a tree without a single ornament on it because… because I'd spent all year running from how I felt and throwing myself into work. So, I made my decision. One more Christmas. Here. As close to them as I can be. And then I'll join them."

He took a deep breath and released it slowly, running his fingers through his hair to push it out of his eyes.

"I'm going to ask you a question now, Sam. One last question. And then, I'll shut up. Heck, I'll even leave if you want me to. You just have to answer it honestly and, whether or not you believe I am who I say I am, I *will* know if you're lying to me."

"You mean it?"

"One hundred percent."

"Not about the lying! About asking one last question and then you'll leave?"

"It'll be like I was never here," Dylan said. "So long as you answer honestly."

She bit her bottom lip and considered the offer a moment before smiling.

"Deal. You Q and I'll A."

"If I were to leave you to your plans…and you use your grandfather's old service revolver to make it as quick and painless as you can—"

The ache she saw behind his eyes made her turn away. She focused instead on the dancing flame in the hearth.

"—what part of Mabel and Sal's Christmas cabin is acceptable to leave stained by your blood? What cherished memories are you okay with being ruined by the horror you leave behind? Your grandmother's quilt on the bed you used to jump into on Christmas morning to wake your parents? No. Maybe the bedroom is too sacred. Maybe here. Where it can redecorate your father's favorite chair…or the landscape Mike painted when she was twelve."

He pointed at it.

"It still hangs above the fireplace. Remnants of your family and the time you spent with them are all around you."

"Stop!"

"Maybe the kitchen, where your mother would spend hours on that ham you liked so much. Or outside along the trail where you and Mike would race each other. Or on the front porch where your dad would smoke his pipe."

"Dylan!"

"Wait until some journalist ties your suicide to your sister's accidental death. The clickbait headlines almost write themselves."

"I get your point, Dylan!"

"I don't think you do. I called your decision selfish before because it is. The only person you are concerned with in this entire transaction is yourself, Sam. If you had done this while your parents were alive—"

"I would never—"

"But if you had, what would they have thought?"

"I can't possibly know."

"Of course, you can. No one knew them like you did. They would have felt they had failed you somehow."

"They didn't!"

"When you see them again, do you think they'll be excited to see you, or will they wonder why you gave up before you made it to the end of your race? Even though you still had your health and your life ahead of you, I mean."

"Without them!"

"Yep. Without them. It sucks. It hurts. It's just how it is. But it isn't forever. If you believed it was, you wouldn't bother with this nonsense. You want to see them again and you will. But you're like a record spinning around and around. You're barely in the first verse, Samantha Cobb, and you want to slap the needle off the wax and call the song over. It isn't. Now, answer my question. What part of your plan honors your mom, your dad, or your sister and the memories they built with you in this place?"

"You still listen to vinyl?"

"Can we stick with the point? Look, I'm shooting straight with you because I know you, Sam."

"You don't."

"I do. And because I know this plan of yours terrifies you nearly as much as it deceives you into believing it's an answer, I'm being far more blunt than I would be if I thought you were broken."

"I'm not broken?"

He gently squeezed her hand and looked her straight in the eyes.

"You're stubborn. You're selfish. And you're short-sighted. I don't think you want to die, Sam, and I think there's plenty of evidence to prove me right. I just think you miss them and can't see past the mountain of pain you're feeling."

She nodded and blinked the tears from of her eyelashes.

"Now…answer my question."

"You know the answer," she said, wiping her eyes with the sleeve of her hoody. "None of it would honor them. I just couldn't see it."

"You couldn't see past your nose. Not being able to see beyond the moment has always been your weakness, but here…in this moment, it could've killed you, Sam. You had a great and wonderful gift. And you mourn the loss of it, which is human. It's right. But it's not all that remains for you."

Samantha shook her head.

"My career has never—"

"And it's never going to."

"To what? What was I going to say?"

"Fulfill you," he said. "It never did and it isn't going to start now."

"So, what then? What big thing is left for me?"

"Big things. Small things. Lots of things. They all matter, Sam. They add up. They make us who we are. If I was allowed to tell you all you stand to miss out on, you'd throw your grandfather's pistol in a hole and bury it."

"Then tell me!"

"I can't. All the things I could tell you aren't promised. They're potential. You still have free will. The same way you could derail them all with a messy bullet to your brainpan, you could also miss out on them by closing yourself off from the world. You could choose paths that steer you clear of them."

"What's the point then?"

"Living. Exploring. Learning. Trying. Being. And loving."

"It sounds…scary. Overwhelming even. Especially doing all that alone."

"Sure. Life is scary. But *this*—inside the story of your life—this is where you can impact things. This is where you have the chance to spread all the love, mercy, and grace you can muster. To be an agent of hope in a hopeless world. Same job as mine, really, just without the travel perks. And I never said you'd have to do it alone."

"I think you're full of it, Dylan Drake."

"You can think so, but I'm right."

"Yeah," she said, falling forward until her head was on his chest. "I think you just might be. Jumping off the merry-go-round is no way to honor all they gave me. And it's not just about making a mess of this place. I don't want to stain their legacy."

Dylan wrapped his arms around her.

Despite her earlier advances, Samantha felt it for what it was: the embrace of her family. A hug sent from somewhere beyond the tiny Christmas cabin. And as she imagined three other sets of arms wrapping around her, she wept and let the pain seep out with every tear that fell.

Samantha awoke on Dylan's chest. They were still on the couch, and he was very much awake. Startled, she sat up straight, an apology perched on her lips.

"It's okay," he said. "You fell asleep. You needed the cry *and* the rest. You've been running from both for far too long."

She reached out and gently touched his cheek.

"I don't know who or what you really are, Dylan,

but I'm thankful I nearly hit you with my car."

He raised an eyebrow and grinned.

"Thanks?"

"I mean…I'm glad you're here with me. That you could speak for Mom, Dad, and Mike."

"They still love you. Death doesn't change that."

"I know. I felt them when I was crying, Dylan. They were calling me to put their love to work. To pour it out on others the way they poured it out for me. And I—"

She suddenly felt awkward having her hand on his face.

"I'm sorry for coming on to you. I was so desperate to feel something. Hell, to feel *anything* other than numb. I made a fool of myself and put you in an awkward position."

"I wasn't offended," Dylan said, stretching his arms over his head. "Just taken. And to be fair, what you needed was a friend, not a…whatever you thought I might be in the moment."

"You're a little young for me anyway."

"Also a factor."

She took a deep breath and let it out slowly. She felt better. Lighter.

"What time is it?"

Dylan checked his watch.

"It's about three minutes till midnight. Nearly

Christmas Day."

"A brand-new day. How should we celebrate?"

"With gifts, of course!"

Her eyes searched his, hoping he was being facetious.

"Gifts?"

"Sure. Why not?"

"I don't have anything for you," she said sheepishly. "You, uh, sort of turned down my best offer."

"How about a promise?"

She smiled at him. It felt like the most genuine thing she'd done in ages.

"Name it."

"I want you to promise, if you ever find yourself doubting your place in this world, you'll call for me. I'd very much like to continue being your friend, Sam, especially since you plan to stick around."

"I won't abandon you," she replied, throwing her arms around his neck. "Not now, not ever!"

She released him from the embrace and asked the question racing through her mind.

"Does that mean I'll see you again?"

"If you call for me, I'll come running. You have my word."

"How?"

"How do you call?"

She nodded.

"Just ask the Author. You may be a bit out of practice, but you know how to reach Him. I'm certain of it."

"You sure you aren't an angel?"

"Nah. Those guys are super serious. I'm…just your friend."

She squeezed him tighter and then let him go.

"It's a deal," she said. "If I ever find myself wanting to give up…"

"Or you get a hankering for my mom's scrambled eggs."

"…I'll say a prayer and wait for you."

His smile made her feel something she hadn't felt since her father's death. Loved.

"What's my gift?"

"Go grab your coat. My gift for you is outside."

"What?"

"You going to doubt me now? After all this? It's verging on insulting, Sam."

She hugged him again.

"Coat. Outside. On it."

"Meet me by the front door."

Snuggled into her coat and her head topped with a red knit hat which had once belonged to her grandfather, Samantha met Dylan at the front door of the cabin. The young man had done nothing to prepare for the weather. He wore the same t-shirt and jeans he had worn for the entirety of his stay.

"You don't have a coat?"

"I don't need one," he said. "Not usually, anyway. I'll be fine."

"Where are we headed?"

"Just outside. But the gift has two parts. The first one is this."

He put a hand on her hip and she winced. The bruise she had felt before was becoming more pronounced. He placed his other hand on her forehead and brushed the hair from her eyes.

Samantha blushed and said, "You know you can't kiss me, right? We've been over this."

Dylan sighed.

"I've never tried to kiss you, Sam. *You* came onto *me*. Now, can you just be still a minute?"

"Okay. Just felt like…you were getting handsy is all."

"Friend," Dylan said, smiling at her. "This love is friend love."

"You're, uh, hands are…very, very warm, friend."

"Shh. I'm listening to my boss."

After a moment, he removed his hands and smiled at her. Samantha knew instantly something had changed.

"Wha…what just happened?"

"I wanted to get rid of the bruises and the remnants of your concussion," he said, putting his hands in the pockets of his jeans. "Thought you'd enjoy your gift better this way. It was the Author's idea. I was just the hands."

"I liked those hands. You know if your girl isn't smart enough to hang onto you—"

"She is. And she'll be happy to hear I made a new friend. You heard that right? *Friend.*"

"Spoilsport."

"Ready for your gift?"

"I'm not sure I can handle much more weird today, Dylan."

"I'll be with you. You'll be okay. I promise."

"I trust you. Lead the way."

Dylan opened the door to the snowy landscape. In the drive, a Bronco sat, dusted with snow and wearing an assortment of icicles.

Samantha stepped out onto the porch and then down the steps.

"That's my…my dad's truck. I sold it after he died. How?"

Dylan placed his hands on Samantha's shoulders and slowly turned her around to face him.

"The Bronco is not the gift."

"What? What's the gift?

Dylan stepped out of the way so she could see the Christmas cabin now adorned in Christmas lights, twinkling in their many colors.

"When did you find time to—"

"I didn't. Sal did."

Dylan pointed to the house and, through the frost covered window, Samantha could just make out the shape of her father as he whirled her mother about in front of the hearth. They were dancing.

"They're up late decorating the tree and making merry," Dylan said. "Mike is wrapping presents and missing you. You had left her a message that morning saying you couldn't make it."

"W-What?"

"Merry Christmas, Sam. Christmas 2017 to be precise. The one you missed. Only…not anymore. The Author didn't care for all the regret lingering from this one day and his editor agreed wholeheartedly. Let's rewrite it, hmm?"

She stared at the window and then looked back at him; her tears already cooled on her cheeks from the frigid air.

"You were the gift they wanted most, Sam. It's my present to them. And to you."

Samantha hugged Dylan so tightly it nearly knocked the young man over.

"I told you I could prove it," he whispered.

She looked back to the window. The dancing was done but through the stillness of the evening came the sound of Sal Cobb's concertina. He was playing "Silent Night" in the calm, sacred way he always played it…as if he and his family were warming themselves by a fire not far from a Bethlehem stable inside of which slept the Christ child in His manger. She knew it really was her Papa behind the frosted glass…celebrating Christmas with his family as he always did. Whoever and whatever Dylan Drake was, he was telling her the truth.

"He always cries." Dylan said.

She looked back at him astonished.

"What did you say?"

"He always cries when he plays "Silent Night." Part of it, I think, is feeling the nearness of the Author. The other part, though, is a deep gratitude for the gifts he's been given. For Mabel, Mike, and his sweet Sam."

"How is this possible?"

"All things are possible for the One writing out your story."

She looked at the cabin and then back to her new

friend, her mind adrift in a sea of questions.

"I told them I couldn't make it. What do I say now?"

"You changed your mind. Tell them you only have today—a brief stopover—but you wouldn't have missed it for anything because it's never been truer. And then cherish the time, Sam. Say all the things you need to. Laugh. Store up joy. Listen to their stories. Have an extra slice of ham. Celebrate all that Christmas means…and be thankful the grace it brought to the world somehow found its way to you when you needed it most."

She touched his face. Again. Dylan's skin didn't feel the slightest bit cold.

"And when the day is over?"

"I'll put you right back where and when we left off. But you'll have had today, Sam…to remember everything you almost threw away. And I believe with all my heart you'll spend the rest of your days trying to carry your family's legacy into every tomorrow, spilling love and laughter out on everyone you meet."

"But what about *your* Christmas? You've already done so much for me. I-I don't want you to miss Christmas with your mom. Not for my sake."

"I won't. I never have before, and I won't start now. Whether I go today or months from now, I'll always be there in time for Christmas. It's the travel perks of the job."

She hugged him again, kissed his cheek, and then wiped her eyes on her coat sleeves.

"My family is really in there? I'm not…I don't know…hallucinating or something?"

"They're in there, Sam. Really and truly."

She believed him, though it all seemed impossible. Somehow, Dylan was all the unimaginable things he claimed to be. She was suddenly quite certain of it.

"I'll never doubt you again," she said, her joy beaming out of her in a smile. "It's the most wonderful gift, Dylan, and I want it more than I've ever wanted anything. I don't know what to say."

"Sure, you do. Of all days, you know exactly what to say today."

"Merry Christmas?"

"Merry Christmas, indeed," he said, watching her walk toward the cabin where her past and future would converge. "And joy the world."

Dylan Drake had walked for miles in the snow, the unfamiliar terrain nearly impossible to navigate by sight alone. Once he turned down the icy road that led further up into the mountain, however, he recognized exactly where he was. There were tracks to follow up the incline and he stayed in them to avoid trudging through the deeper powder. Less than a mile from the cabin, he noted the scarred tree—its wound the reminder of an unfortunate encounter with a tumbling vehicle.

The cabin itself looked much the same as he remembered it. The 4x4 parked in front of it, however, was new. On the porch, he brushed the snow from his shoes to be sure he wouldn't track the weather in with him. And then he knocked.

Sam looked the same as he remembered her save for the strands of gray in her hair and a few lines around her eyes. The smile on her face upon seeing him proved contagious.

"Dylan Drake," she said, throwing her arms around him. "You got my call."

"I did," he said, hugging her back. "Merry Christmas, Sam."

"Come in out of the snow," she said. "Meet the family."

He followed her into the Christmas Cabin (as her parents had dubbed it long ago) where a fire in the hearth instantly began to combat the chill in his bones. The Christmas tree had already been decorated with silver tinsel and vintage glass ornaments, and the smell of warm apple cider filled the place.

"Kids!" Sam called. "Honey! We've got company!"

No sooner did the words leave her lips than two girls rushed to their mother's side, staring up at the strange man standing next to her. The older of the two, blonde with dark brown eyes, smiled at Dylan timidly. She was missing one of her front teeth. The younger, with her chestnut hair and green eyes, pulled at her mother's hand until Samantha lifted her to her hip.

"Dylan, I'd like you to meet my daughters," Sam said, placing a hand on the older girl's head. "This is Mikela and this little thing on my hip is Mabel Jo."

"Named after two equally lovely ladies," Dylan said, dropping to one knee so that he could look Mikela in the eyes. "It's nice to meet you, Mikela. My name is Dylan."

He raised up a little to Mabel Jo's height and smiled at her.

"Hello, Mabel Jo. I'm Dylan. It's nice to meet you, too."

As he stood, he couldn't help but chuckle.

"What?" Sam asked.

"Mike and Jo," he said. "You just couldn't help yourself, could you?"

"The Tennessee Terrors live on," she said. "Go back and play, girls. Momma needs to chat with Mr. Dylan."

They watched as the girls ran back toward the only bedroom.

"Honey?" Sam called again.

"I heard you, dear," a man shouted from the kitchen. "Just filling some mugs of Christmas cheer."

As the man stepped back into the main room, he had to duck lest he hit his head on the door frame. He carried three steaming mugs on a small tray. Despite his lumberjack physique, there was a gentleness to him that was clear by the way he carried himself.

"Dylan, this is my husband, Clayton Holbeck," Sam said.

"Friends call me Clay," the large man clarified, offering his hand to Dylan.

"It's good to meet you, Clay," Dylan replied as he shook it.

"Hot apple cider," Clay said, holding a mug out for him. "It's Sam's mother's recipe."

"Thank you."

"Should help take the chill off."

Clay handed a mug to Sam and then set the tray down on the coffee table before claiming the last mug for himself.

"I'm going to go play Chutes and Ladders with the girls," Clay said, "so you two can catch up."

"Thanks, babe," Sam said. "You're the best."

Dylan took a sip of the cider and sighed. Not only was it as delicious as it smelled, but the mug made short work of warming his hands. When he glanced over at Sam, she was looking him up and down, scrutinizing.

"Something wrong?"

"You look younger," she said. "Exactly how old are you, Dylan Drake?"

"20-ish. About the same as the last time I saw you."

"Wrong. The last time I saw you, you were edging 30. And you had a lot of tattoos, which surprised me."

"Interesting. When was that?"

"Four years ago last March."

"That wasn't me," he replied. "Or, at least, it wasn't this me. I haven't seen you since you nearly hit me with your car."

"That's not possible."

"I don't doubt that you saw me, Sam."

"Of course, I saw you. Just like now…I called, and you came…although I was in New York at the time."

"Wherever and whenever. Sure. But that was some other me from further down the line. A me older than I am now."

"Well, that's deeply confusing."

"Welcome to my world."

"No, thanks. I like mine just fine the way it is."

"You *have* built a nice life for yourself. Congratulations."

Her eyes narrowed.

"Go ahead. Say you told me so. I deserve it."

"No. You don't. I'm happy for you. Do you, uh, mind if I sit, though? It was a long walk up here in the cold."

"Oh, my gosh! I totally didn't think. Yes, yes. Sit. But first—"

She threw her arms around his neck and squeezed tight before planting a sisterly kiss on his cheek.

"I missed you," she said, pointing toward what had once been her father's chair.

He sat and smiled back at her.

"It's good to be missed, actually. I'm sorry that being friends with me means going long stretches without contact."

"Comes with your job," she replied after a sip of cider. "And, like I said, you came last time I called, too. So, catch me up on your life. Is your special someone still in the picture?"

"She is," he said, unable to stop the smile spreading across his face.

"What's she like?"

"Crazy. And kind. Brave. Smart."

"All things she'd have to be to be a suitable match for you, kiddo. Are you going to make an honest woman of her?"

There was a sadness in his eyes that made Sam ache for her friend. Though he didn't answer her question, she thought it best to leave the topic altogether.

"I appreciate you, Dylan. There was never a doubt

in my mind that you'd come."

"I'm pleased to see you again, Sam. It does my heart good. But I assumed you didn't reach out for a social call. Did you need something?"

"Not for me, no. But there's a man I know who could really use your help."

"Okay."

"And I know what you're going to say, Dylan. I can't just call on you to fix things for other people, but—"

"Sam, I'm your friend. There aren't limits on that. If it's within my power and authority to help, I will."

She smiled at him.

"You sweet boy."

"Pardon?"

"I'm just struck by the sameness of you, is all. Rock steady. Stalwart. This is the you that I remember."

"The other me not so much?"

"Oh, I saw you in him, for certain. And your kindness was still a warm glow behind his eyes. But there was something dangerous about him, too. Like the world had been unkind and he was wounded but trying not to let it corrupt him. It worried me, to be honest."

"I…yeah, I think I understand who you met."

"It was you."

"After a fashion, yes. Me and not me. All at once."

"That's ridiculous."

Dylan raised an eyebrow and Samantha laughed.

"But ridiculous is your stock and trade," she said, nodding. "I should remember that."

"Who needs my help, Sam?"

"A man named Chester Wheatland. I've known him since I was a kid. He was friends with my dad. We lost touch for quite some time but reconnected a year or so after you and I met. He's done a fair bit of work for Clay and I over the past few years."

"You've moved to charitable work, I read."

"Checking up on me, Dylan?"

"I don't really do social media," he replied, "but I have higher connections."

"Chester is the closest thing to a saint I've ever met, present company excluded. But, like all of us, he lives with certain regrets. Chief among them is abandoning a pregnant girlfriend 40 years ago. Recently, Chester got a grim diagnosis. Despite all the good he's done for my family and the less fortunate, he couldn't shake the shame he was hanging onto."

"Did he try to find his old flame?"

"That's why I called you. Yesterday, he learned that she had passed away. She never returned his calls or letters, so he doesn't know what became of the child. Now, maybe she never gave birth. Her obituary listed children, but they were too young to have been Chester's.

She could've been pressured into an abortion. Especially back then. Mixed race couples weren't exactly accepted. It's also possible she could've had a miscarriage."

"Or put the child up for adoption."

"But those records would be sealed," Sam said. "I already made a few calls. I got no traction, Dylan, and you know how tenacious I can be. Without her alive to tell him what happened—"

"I get it. I'm not sure how much I'll be allowed to help, Sam. I'll have to ask."

"No, I get it. But I felt it down deep…that I should call for you, I mean. That I should ask for help."

"I'm glad you did. And you know I'll do what I can. But, depending on what happened 40 years ago, there may not be a happy ending to this story. There isn't always."

"I know. And I know that we live, and we die. We win, lose, hope, regret. All of it. I'm not asking you to heal Chester's cancer the way you healed my hip years ago."

"I didn't fix your hip, Sam. My boss did."

"You know what I mean, though. I'm not asking you to change any of the story that's already happened."

"You want me to find his kid."

"If there's a kid, yes."

Dylan nodded, scratching at his chin.

"Research is my thing," he admitted. "That and the occasional bit of swordplay. I can find out what happened—for good or ill. But then what?"

"The truth can hurt," she replied, a sad smile on her face. "I didn't want to hear the truth you brought to me that Christmas when I almost threw it all away. But I needed to hear it and…well, you brought it to me in a way that didn't take away my loss or my mourning but gave me a reason to press on anyway. With hope. With a plan to take the blessings that had been piled on top of me and pour them out on others. And I have, Dylan. And Chester…he's been a real part of that."

"Just because I haven't been around doesn't mean I don't keep up with you, Sam. You've loved well. You've served well. Your parents and Mike…they'd be so proud."

"Chester isn't dead yet." A single tear dripped from her left eye and Sam wiped it away with the back of her sleeve before taking a deep breath and continuing. "He's got ahead of him whatever time is left. I just don't want him spending that time—"

"Eaten up with regret. I get that. But, Sam, even if I find a child out there—even if I can bring him hope—there's no guarantee that he'll let go of that regret. We can't save everyone."

"I know. And I know that his free will means he can have an open path to joy and still retreat into sorrow.

I know it all too well. I've done it. But then you came. If I didn't believe you were his best chance, I wouldn't have called. Chester needs a miracle, Dylan. More than that, he needs a friend the way I needed one that dark, hopeless night. He needs you. No matter where this journey leads."

Dylan nodded and smiled at her. She was the same Samantha Cobb he had met on that long-ago Christmas, but she was free and at peace. He liked her even more than he had then.

"Stop smiling at me," she said, winking at him. "I'm a married woman, I'll have you know."

"Really?"

"Sorry. Old habits."

"To be fair," Clay said from the door, "she told me up front she planned to flirt with you. She said she gets a laugh out of how uncomfortable it makes you."

"I'm so glad my discomfort entertains you, Sam."

"I'm a simple woman with simple pleasures. Chutes and Ladders over already, hon?"

"No, but the girls drained my Apple Cider dry. Figured a refill was in order. Dylan, can I warm your cup?"

"I'm good, thanks," Dylan said. "And I should go. Seems I have a bit of homework if I'm going to help Chester."

"Oh, don't go," Sam pleaded. "The girls brought

sleeping bags and are camping in the bedroom with me and Clay. You can have the lumpy couch and spend Christmas Eve with us. I'll call Chester tonight and tell him you need a ride to…let's say…*Texas*. You can celebrate with us in the morning and then hit the road with him after breakfast."

"I don't—"

"Stay, Dylan," Clayton added. "I'm not sure I believe half the things I've heard about you, but you're something of a legend in our little family. And I know that, what I have now, I owe largely to your intervention. So, stay. As far as we're concerned, you're family. Where else would you go for Christmas?"

"Please," Sam said. "It would mean a lot to me."

Dylan thought for a moment and then smiled.

"I do love a good lumpy couch."

"Alright," Clay said, slapping him on the shoulder. "I'll make it up for you after the kids are down."

"And we've got bread pudding in the oven," Sam said, "so dessert awaits you."

"I think you're forgetting something," Clay said, pointing toward the tree.

Sam's eyes widened.

"How did I forget?"

"Forget what?" Dylan asked.

"I have a gift for you," Sam said, digging through

the wrapped packages under the tree. "I've been holding onto it since just after I saw you last."

"Sam, you didn't need to—"

"Don't step on this moment," Clay whispered. "She's been *so* excited to give this to you."

Dylan smiled at the large man and nodded.

"Found it!"

Sam brought Dylan a small box wrapped in a lovely blue paper marked with images of angels.

The young man raised an eyebrow as he looked back to Sam.

"Inside joke," she said.

"It's Christmas Eve," he reminded. "Shouldn't I open this tomorrow?"

"Open it now," Clay said. "Like she said, she's been holding onto it for a few years now."

Dylan carefully unwrapped the paper and opened the small box to discover a tiny cross pin attached to a memo card upon which was written: Psalm 34:19.

"I know cross pins are a dime a dozen," Sam said, "but that one is special."

"She had it made especially for you," Clay added.

Dylan grinned awkwardly, examining the cross.

"I feel like I'm missing something."

"I had it made from the bullet."

Dylan looked up at his friend whose smile melted

away any chill that remained in his bones.

"The bullet from——?"

"I wanted you to remember," she said, "what you and your boss did for me that night."

"What you did for me and the girls, too," Clay said.

"The pin is just my way of sticking close to my friend. On the toughest Christmas of my life, Dylan, you proved I wasn't alone. I wanted you to know that you're never alone, either. Not really. Our love, our hope, and our prayers follow after you. And, after seeing that other, older version of you, I wanted you to remember who you are. To me. And I'm sure to so many others."

"I-I don't know what to say, Sam."

"Sure, you do. Of all days, you know exactly what to say today."

He smiled and then hugged her.

"Merry Christmas, Sam."

"Easy, tiger. My husband in right there."

"Sam!"

"She's messing with both of us," Clay said. "It's her way."

"You're not wrong," Sam said, giving her husband a wink. "Now, let's check on that bread pudding, yeah?"

THE ROAD TO CHRISTMAS

Chester Whealtand was loading his worn overnight bag behind the seat of his F150 extended cab when he caught sight of the young man approaching with a duffle bag. He hadn't wanted any company on this drive but, when his good friends Clay and Sam Holbeck had asked him for a favor, Chester couldn't really decline. They had done too much for him over the years to be denied.

"Are you Mr. Chester Wheatland?" the young man asked.

"Since the day I was born. You're Dylan, I take it."

"Dylan Drake…yes, sir. Sam and Clay called ahead, I see."

"They said you needed a ride to the Lone Star state."

"Yes, sir. They said you were about to make a road trip to Louisiana and thought you might get me that far and I could split the gas with you."

"I don't need your gas money, son. And to be frank, I don't much care for dragging a stranger all those miles… especially on Christmas Day. But if Sam Holbeck vouches for someone, they're good enough for me. Just throw your bag behind the seat and let's get on the road."

Dylan did as he was asked and then climbed into the passenger seat. The truck, older than Dylan's 20 years of age, was as well-preserved as the man who owned it. Bald and clean-shaven, Chester had likely looked roughly the same for many years. There was a youthfulness in the elder man's energy belying the wrinkles beneath his eyes and the liver spots dotting the back of his calloused hands. Focused as he was on the task before him, he had driven Dylan more than 30 miles down the road before he spoke again.

"Mind if I ask how you know the Holbecks, son?"

"I only recently met Clay," Dylan admitted, "but

I've known Sam for a long time."

"As young as you are, you ain't known anybody a *long* time."

Dylan chuckled politely.

"You'd be surprised, Mr. Wheatland. Sam and I go back a good 10 years…since before she was a Holbeck."

Chester shook his head.

"You must've been just a sprout then. How'd you meet?"

"She nearly hit me with her car."

Chester looked over at Dylan as amazed as if the young man had grown a second head right before his eyes.

"I swear. She swerved to miss me and rolled her rental."

"That was you? Pulled her out of the wreckage and up to her cabin?"

"Seemed the thing to do at the time."

Chester glanced over at the young man, giving him the once-over.

"So, you're the mystery man. Samantha Holbeck's guardian angel."

"I've certainly been called worse."

"Ain't we all. What takes you all the way to Texas?"

"Got a few folks to check on before the new year begins. Flights can be expensive and…well, Sam and Clay thought you and I would get along just fine. They speak highly of you.”

“You can’t kid a kidder. They were worried about me driving so far alone and thought they’d help us both out. Sorry I can’t get you closer than Shreveport, young man, but they’ve got buses that go from there into Texas. Shouldn’t be too difficult for ya provided you’ve got a bit of cash.”

“What takes you to Louisiana, Mr. Wheatland? Sam said something about a family obligation.”

Chester shook his head, eyes fixed on the road ahead.

“More like regret from dodging obligations. But I don’t want to get into all that.”

“Yessir.”

“And you can stop the ‘Sir’ business. I appreciate your manners, son, but if we’re sharing this ride for a long haul, it’s best you call me Chester like most other folks.”

“Then please feel free to call me Dylan.”

“Will do.”

“Are you hungry, Chester? I packed some granola bars in my bag in case either of us needed some nourishment.”

“Ain’t never thought of no granola bar as nourishment, son, but I appreciate the offer. If I get hungry enough, I'll get me a greasy spoon burger. You appreciate a good burger, Dylan?"

Dylan smiled. He liked Chester.

"I've been known to, yes."

"Well, I know all the best spots. Come lunch time, I'll find us something mean and memorable. How about?"

"Sounds good. But, if you aren't letting me chip in for the gas, I'd like your burger to be my treat."

Chester laughed.

"Ain't never been one to turn down free food, son. I guess that'll do just fine. Hmm-mm. Yes, sir, a burger sounds mighty good. Maybe even a nice big order of onion rings, too."

"With a Coke float to wash it all down?"

"No, sir. A chocolate shake. Made with Bosco and 'nilla ice cream like I like 'em. Yes, sir. That's a meal fit for a king right there. And I know just where we can get it."

"It sounds like a plan, Chester. And a tasty one, too."

Lunch in Memphis proved to be as good as Chester had promised and both men decided lingering over their milkshakes and letting their food settle was the wisest course of action. Opposite one another in a small, kitschy booth, Chester Wheatland stirred his chocolate shake round and round with a straw. Dylan pulled a small book from the sport coat he wore and retrieved a pen from his interior pocket.

"You some kind of writer?" Chester asked.

"Oh, no. But I journal quite a bit when I'm traveling."

"It's a diary then?"

"Yeah. Basically. You keep one?"

"Nah. Ain't never seen much need. My memory is still sharp, and I never was much good with spelling things. Reading neither. I got me the whatever-you-call-it. Where you see things all a-jumble and the like."

"Dyslexia?"

"Yeah, that's the one. O' course they had no name for it back when I was schooling. They just passed me on along 'cause they was sick o' looking at me, I suppose. You gonna write about this trip?"

"Eventually," Dylan said. "Right now, though, I'm writing a letter."

"An actual letter, eh? I didn't think young men your age did anything but the texting."

"I don't keep a phone, actually. And writing a letter is much more personal."

"You writing to family?"

"No, sir. I'm writing to the girl I…well, I guess you'd say—"

"You love her," Chester said. He then laughed so hard and loud it drew the attention of every patron in the diner. "You should've seen your eyes light up, boy! You got it bad. Ol' Chester can tell. You been got by Cupid's bow and arrows. Shot full of 'em from the look of ya."

Dylan smiled, his mind conjuring an image of the woman he loved.

"She's very special."

"Good for you," Chester said, taking a long, slow drag on his straw. "You got plans to marry?"

"Not currently. My job keeps me moving from place to place. I don't think this sort of life would be very fair to her."

"She love you anything close to what's radiating off of you?"

"For some reason, yes."

"Then being apart ain't ever gonna get better. Best just to make a life for yourself while you're still young enough to manage it. You ain't getting any younger, boy. It don't work that way for anyone."

Dylan set the pen down and looked at his new friend.

"Have you ever been in love, Chester?"

"Oh, sure. Plenty of times. Mostly with all the wrong women, but with a few of the right ones, too. Got myself married to one of the good ones. Had 23 years with my Delia before the cancer took her."

Dylan could see the pain in his eyes, as suddenly fresh for the elderly man as if she had died mere hours earlier.

"I'm sorry."

"For what? I wouldn't take those 23 years back for anything. And, sure, I miss her—more fiercely some days than others—but it's only 'cause I had me a good woman to miss. You can't really miss what you ain't been blessed enough to have, ya know."

"There's a lot of wisdom in your perspective. Did you have children?"

"We tried but Delia's body just couldn't bear any babies. Our road to parenthood didn't lead nowhere but heartache."

Dylan nodded, unsure of what to say. Chester went back to his shake. The waitress, a matronly woman named Sue, left the bill and the young man paid her with enough cash that she was left with a sizable tip.

"Chester?"

Chester looked up from his shake.

"How did you know Delia was the one?"

Chester smiled and then thought for a moment before answering.

"It was in my bones," he said. "My love for her. My devotion. It was rooted down so deep inside me nothing else made any kind of sense at all. When I imagined my future, she was always there. I couldn't shake it. I'd have given up anything I had claim to just to make her mine. Why'd you ask? You wondering if your gal is the one for you?"

"Not really. I know she is. But sometimes you doubt yourself, you know? Even the best among us make poor choices or play the fool on occasion. Often, we need to hear someone else say what we already know. Sometimes it's easier to believe a stranger than it is to trust ourselves."

"Amen to that," Chester replied. "I was watching a preacher the other night on the YouTube talking how there ain't nobody lies to us more than we lie to ourselves."

"I believe it. I think the thing we most need saving from is ourselves—our own inclinations and impulses."

"You believe in God, Dylan?"

Dylan smiled and nodded.

"I do."

"Then, far as He's concerned, we're brothers, right?"

"Yessir."

"I thought we covered the 'sir' business."

"Sorry, Chester. Old habits."

"It's a good one. But given how much love we get from the Holbecks—and how much we've got for them—we were practically family anyhow. Our faith takes it a step further. Such being the case, I'll tell you something I ain't told a great many."

Chester leaned across the small table and whispered.

"I've got the cancer, son. And I ain't long for this hard old world if them doctors are as good as their word."

"I'm sorry, Chester. Truly."

"Ain't nothin' for it. It's gone too far for any treatments or such. What time I got left is what time I got left. Simple and sad, but the truth all the same."

"Then I have to assume this trip is pretty important to you."

Chester narrowed his eyes, searching Dylan's for a moment before he spoke again.

"You got a way about you, Dylan. A perception. I look in your eyes and see a lot more than the 20-something years you're wearing on your bones. The only way a man your age gains that sort of wisdom is through a lot of hard-fought experience. You've seen a lot, haven't you, son?"

"More than my share, yes."

"You got any hope left?"

"And grace to spare," Dylan said with a nod.

"I could use a bit of both, truth be told. I ain't fond of my odds."

"Of?"

"Finding the truth."

"About?"

"I'll tell you more in the truck," Chester said. "We need to get some miles under us before nightfall. I'm gonna hit the head and then we'll roll out."

"I'll meet you outside."

Chester and Dylan were traveling though Forest City, Arkansas when the oil light on the dashboard of Chester's truck began to glow a menacing orange. He pulled off on the side of the road and popped the hood. When he wandered around to the passenger door, Dylan knew it likely wasn't good news.

"Spilling all my oil," Chester said. "Ain't gonna limp into the next town at this rate. Engine's already overheating. Could crack my engine block if I'm not careful."

"How did it happen?"

"Couldn't tell ya. I gave everything under the hood

a once-over before we left Nashville. Didn't see a thing out of place."

"So, what's the plan?"

"Well, Arkansas ain't got any roadside assistance. Best I can do is call for a tow. But it's going to cost us."

"I can chip in."

"Ain't the money that irks me, son. It's the time. Loretta's funeral is tomorrow. If I'm to talk to her kin—"

"What are the options? Rent a new vehicle?"

"Them rental folks want a credit card," Chester said. "Ain't never had one. Don't believe in 'em. Seen too many sink into debt by mismanaging such things."

"I don't have one either, I'm afraid."

"Then we're sunk, Dylan."

"If we can get to Shreveport tomorrow," the young man said, "I can help you hunt down whatever information we can find."

"I appreciate your kindness, son, but the odds of my learning much were already long."

"Never say never. Like you said, Chester…we're family. If you need a hand, I'll lend it. For as long as you need."

Chester reached through the rolled down window and patted the boy on his right shoulder.

"You're a good egg, Dylan. That's how my Delia would've put it. She'd have liked you, boy. Yes, sir. She'd have thought you were quite the fella. You'd have liked her, too. Sweet as a baby's laugh, my Delia."

"I'm sorry I never had the pleasure."

"When this long ol' road is past us, son, and we meet up again in our forever home, I'll be sure to introduce you."

"One more reason to be homesick," Dylan said with a smile.

"Gather our gear, son. I'll call for a tow. Maybe we can find a cheap place to bed down for the night and get some grub."

"You've got room after the lunch we had?"

"It'll take a hot minute for a tow and to find a motel. Come then, you'll be ready again, too. I guarantee."

After a $150 tow to a garage that wouldn't open until early the next morning, Chester and Dylan settled in a cheap, local motel in a room with two double beds. After stowing their bags, they walked the three-quarters of a mile to the roadside diner recommended by the tow truck driver. It's dim neon sign read: Topper's…Home of the Rolland.

Their waitress, a young woman not much older than Dylan, greeted them with a sweet smile.

"Good evening, gentlemen. My name is Abby and I'll be your server tonight. What can I start you off with?"

"Water for me," Dylan replied.

"Black coffee."

"Will you need cream and sugar?"

Chester looked across the booth to Dylan and winked before looking back up at the young waitress.

"If I wanted cream and sugar, miss, I wouldn't be drinking my coffee black."

"I see your point," Abby said with a smile. "I guess I was on automatic pilot. I've got Christmas on my mind more than anything else. You two ready to order or you need a minute?"

Dylan raised his hand. Abby raised her eyebrows.

"I was wondering what a 'Rolland' is."

"It's a grilled chicken slider on a yeast roll," Abbey explained. "It comes topped with pepper jack cheese, bacon, and onion jam."

"So, it's called a 'Rolland' because of the roll?"

"And on account of it being the creation of Roland Topper, the owner. It's sort of a play on words."

"Sort of," Chester agreed.

"They come two to a platter with fries and your choice of side salad, slaw, or carrot salad."

"I'll take the Rolland," Dylan decided, "and I'll have the side salad with ranch dressing."

"Same for me but with the carrot salad," Chester added. "Ain't had a good carrot salad in many a year."

"Ours it pretty bumpin'," Abby replied. "You won't be disappointed. I'll get your order in and be right back with your drinks."

After the waitress was gone, Chester leaned closer to Dylan and whispered.

"Bumping? Is that a good thing?"

Dylan laughed.

"I guess you'll find out."

Chester laughed, too, and then began humming along to the Christmas music piped through the speakers in the old diner. The owners had strung silver tinsel and placed a decorated tree near the register.

'Not exactly Sam's Christmas cabin,' Dylan thought, 'but it could be worse.'

"Can I ask you a question, Chester?"

"Ain't got nowhere to go. Might as well."

"I was just wondering what you do for the Holbecks."

"Drive mostly. I deliver men that need work to the jobs Clay sets 'em up with. I taxi single moms to get their young ones to the doctor. I drop supplies to some of the shelters that Sam fights to keep open. All the work they do with their ministry…and make no mistake that 'charity' of theirs is really a ministry…but all that work requires people willing to serve. Most of their crew is folks they helped that want to pay it forward and whatnot. But me…well, after Delia passed, I didn't have any place better to be. I thought serving alongside them might do my soul some good. It certainly gave me something to put my mind to aside from my grieving. I got to know Sam and Clay…the work they were doing and, more importantly, the heart they were doing it with—"

He paused as if trying to think of how best to word it.

"And you recognized family." Dylan offered.

Chester slapped the table and pointed a finger at Dylan.

"They don't just give their time or their effort, though they give a considerable amount o' both. It's themselves they give most of all. Their love and their joy and all the good they get hold of. They can't help themselves, Dylan. They just keep pouring it out on folks."

"Sam's folks were the same, I'm told. She comes by it honestly. I'm glad Clay is built of the same stuff."

"I'd do anything for them folks," Chester admitted. "Even drag a skinny white boy across half the country."

"Don't exaggerate, Chester. We only made it to Arkansas."

Chester laughed and shook his head.

"I ain't happy either, son, I can assure you. And since you've heard my story and my shame, you know why."

Dylan took a deep breath and let it out slow. He had followed his instincts and intervened. The rest would be up to the Author.

"Why are you hanging onto shame, Chester? Don't you know you're already forgiven?"

"Oh, sure. I know God forgave me long ago. Forgotten about it already…so the good book says. But Loretta Jones—she's the old flame who passed away—she ain't ever had the chance to forgive me 'cause I wasn't man enough to face her. And our baby, if our baby ever came to be born, ain't forgiven me. I abandoned my responsibilities, Dylan. Ain't no lower a man can go."

"We all have things in our past we'd do differently if we had them to do over again, Chester. Fixating on them doesn't do anyone any good. We can only do the best we can in any given situation. The man you are today wouldn't make the same choice, so he shouldn't bear the guilt. The Chester Wheatland who ran away was buried many years ago and his sins long since forgiven."

"I ain't forgiven myself, though, boy. And I ain't so sure I can."

"You can't change the past. All you can do is your

best today. And I get it. Heading to Shreveport was part of doing your best now."

"Yet here we sit," Chester said. "Loretta's funeral was my best chance of finding out the truth. Even if they have us on the road by 9 a.m. tomorrow, we ain't about to make her service in Shreveport."

"One water," Abby said, placing Dylan's glass down with a mug of piping hot coffee. "And a black coffee. "I forgot to ask you both if you wanted your salads before the rest of your meal."

"Yes, please," Chester said.

"That would be great, thanks, Abby," Dylan added.

"No problem. Let me get my other table some re-fills and I'll be back with salads."

As she walked away, Dylan looked out of the window next to him, watching the 18-wheelers flying by on the highway less than half a mile away.

"You got family, son?"

Dylan turned back to his new friend and nodded.

"My mom lives outside Chicago. I get back there whenever I can."

"You don't live at home anymore?"

"I do, but I move around a lot. The work I do can be done most anywhere, so there's not much reason to stay in one place. But I get back home as often as I can. She seldom notices I've been gone."

"She notices," Chester said. "Mommas always notice. She's just letting you soar."

"I wouldn't be me without her. My dad died before I was born. She had to wear a lot of hats to keep us afloat. We had other folks around. Friends and community. Even a few people who had been close to my dad. But it was still tough on her sometimes."

"Therein's my shame, Dylan. I put someone else through those hard, sorrowful times. Your dad didn't abandon you. He died. I've got no such excuse."

"You were a kid who panicked, Chester."

"I was 23. That ain't no kid. It isn't now and it certainly wasn't back then."

Abby returned to the table with their salads and grinned at how excited Chester seemed to be over his.

"You aren't going to be disappointed," she said. "It's a local favorite."

The look on Chester's face as he took his first bite proved her point.

"Abby," Dylan said, "Do you mind if I ask you a question?"

"Shoot," the girl said.

"If you messed up—and I mean really messed up in a way that cost more than just you—do you think after 40 years have passed you'd still feel guilty?"

Abby crossed her arms and thought for a minute.

"And here I thought you were going to ask me about desserts or something."

"Sorry."

"No. It's…an interesting question. I think no. I mean, sure, you hate to disappoint people. But I haven't met a person yet who wasn't messy to one degree or another. Everyone has skeletons. Everyone has let someone down. We're just humans, after all, and making a mess of things comes pretty natural to us all."

"You a church-going gal, Abby?" Chester asked.

"Yes, sir. In fact, as soon as I blow out of here tonight, I'm headed there. My pastor likes to spend Christmas night singing hymns by candlelight."

"Why Christmas night and not Christmas Eve?" Dylan asked.

"Everybody celebrates on Christmas Eve and Christmas morning. But, after all the presents are open and everyone's had their fill of pumpkin pie and such, most folks just turn their eyes and hearts back toward the day-to-day of life. We choose to sing on Christmas night. It's our way of remembering what we've been celebrating and, hopefully, carrying God's great love with us into all the days to follow."

"I like that," Chester said, dabbing at the corner of his mouth with his napkin.

"So do I," Dylan added. "I don't suppose you've

got room for two strangers, do you?"

"Always," Abby replied with a smile. "We meet at 11 p.m. down at Calvary Road Baptist."

"We're not from around here. We're just staying the night because Chester's truck broke down on our way through the area."

"You two staying down at the Teardrop Inn?"

"How'd you guess?"

Abby chuckled.

"It's the only motel within walking distance. I'll tell you what. If you're serious about coming out to sing, I can swing by there and give you a lift to the church."

"Your momma might not want you giving rides to strangers," Chester warned.

"My momma will be with me," Abby said. "My kid brother, too."

"Are you sure you don't mind?" Dylan asked.

"It's Christmas. What's to mind?"

"You're awfully kind," Chester said. "I'm certainly game if the boy is."

"Sold," Dylan said, "providing you'll let me pay you something for your trouble."

"Put it in the collection plate," Abby said. "All donations tonight are going toward a new organ for the church."

"It's a deal. Thanks, Abby."

"My pleasure. Let me go check on your food and swing by my other tables. Back in a shake."

"Sweet girl," Chester said once Abby was out of earshot.

"Yep."

"About your age, too."

"I have someone," Dylan reminded.

"She must be a real dandy."

"Saved my life. Literally."

"Come again?"

"It's a long story, Chester. And not one I'd care to repeat at the moment. It's still Christmas and my mind is on better days."

"You're a strange kid, if you don't mind me sayin'."

"You're not the first to say so."

"You've got a lifetime's worth of stories behind those young eyes o' yours. I confess I feel a certain kinship with you, Dylan. One I don't normally feel with folks your age."

"I'm always keen to make a new friend," Dylan replied. "I think Sam sort of assumed we'd hit it off."

"She and Clay both have a way with people. Always convincing folks to step out of where they've grown too comfortable and help folks who wouldn't know comfort from nothin'. Did you know her when she was in the business world?"

"Not really. But I know she felt unfulfilled."

"I knew her folks when she and her sister were just kids. Lost touch long before they passed. I reconnected with Sam when I was working a construction job. Too much work for an old man, but I was determined. Saw Sam trying to talk some poor brother living on the street into escorting her to lunch. She made it seem like he'd be doing her a favor. Like she didn't know the area and needed someone to keep her from wandering down the wrong street or something. It really struck me, son, the way she made herself all about *his* dignity. And I mean, a world more about it than he was himself. The man ain't had a decent bath or a change o' clothes in the two weeks I'd been working that site. But you'd have thought he was her long, lost daddy the way she talked to him."

"Maybe that's her secret. Maybe she sees the people she helps like they're the family she's lost. As though, by treating people with mercy and grace, she's somehow re-paying all the love she grew up with."

"You knew her family? How old are you?"

"I know of them. So much so it feels like I knew them. Sadly, they were gone before I first met Sam."

"You mean before she tried to run you down."

"She wasn't trying to r—Look the road was icy and she had no control."

Chester took a sip of his coffee and winked at

the boy. Dylan simply shook his head. Both men turned their attention to their salads and then to the meals Abby dropped at their table. The "Rolland" proved to be quite delicious and both men cleaned their plates.

"I'm sorry we didn't make it to Shreveport," Dylan said just after Abby cleared their table of the empty plates.

"Me, too. Maybe it's God's way of saying it's too late to fix my mistake and I just have to live with the consequences."

"Maybe. Or maybe, He's at work in other ways and the answers weren't really in Shreveport."

"I suppose I'll be able to ask Him myself soon enough."

Dylan searched the older man's eyes before saying, "If there was some way I could take your burden from you, I would, Chester."

"Perish the thought, son. I've lived a long enough time. The good book says God knew us before He formed us in our mothers' wombs. I reckon that means He also knows when we're going to pass. It's a day I've been headed toward since I drew my first breath. I ain't scared o' dyin'. I'll see my Delia again. I'll meet my Savior and see my momma. It's the stuff of rejoicing, if you ask me."

Dylan smiled, thankful for the moment.

"I like you, Chester. If I was meant to spend Christmas Day on the road, I'm grateful it was by your side.

Somehow, it feels like my own story would be a bit worse off if I hadn't met you."

"That's mighty kind, Dylan. When you get to be my age, you've already seen too many friends pass on. While I know I'll get to see them again, it's still good for my soul to make a new one from time to time."

"Agreed. You ready to walk off this meal?"

"Yes, I am. Would like to grab me a shower, too, before young Miss Abby picks us up for the singing."

Both men settled the bill and said their goodbyes to Abby, promising to be ready when she came by the motel to pick them up. Chester was quiet on the walk back to the Teardrop Inn and Dylan felt he knew why.

"You know, I'll still ride with you to Shreveport once the truck is fixed. But I also understand if you just want to head back home."

"I guess I'll sleep on it, and we'll see what the mechanic says tomorrow before I make my decision. Wouldn't feel right not getting you down the road, though."

"Don't worry about me," Dylan said. "I've got plenty of ways to get where I need to be."

"Still, I was rather enjoying the ride. The company alone might make it worth continuing on."

"Whatever you decide, Chester."

The motel room was sparse but clean and both men had time to shower and change before Abby arrived. As promised, she picked them up with her mother, Angela Benson, and her younger brother, Shaun, already in the car. After quick introductions were made, Abby drove them 5 miles or so to Calvary Road Baptist Church where parking was surprisingly hard to come by around the small, brick church. Inside, in a sanctuary which seemed like it had not been updated since the mid-1950s, the wooden pews were packed with smiling parishioners, many bedecked—not unlike the halls—in holiday finery. At the front, near the altar and the pulpit, a nativity scene was set upon what was normally the communion table.

For nearly an hour, they sang Christmas hymns before the pastor of the church, a 40-something man named Darren Pitney, stood up to read a selection from Luke chapter 2. When he was finished, they closed the service with "O Holy Night," which somehow rose from the mediocre voices of the crowd to become an angelic choir. As Dylan closed his eyes, he could almost imagine the frightened shepherds gazing up at the multitude of heavenly hosts. It comforted him to think of the reconciliation which began that night so long ago.

At the close of the service, Dylan and Chester waited for Abby's mother, Angela, who was in a spirited conversation with a group of women. Shaun, Abby's younger brother by 7 years, proved to be as pleasant to talk to as his sister, and both men enjoyed the sense of community they felt among the congregation. At some point, as he engaged Shaun in small talk, Dylan lost sight of Chester. When the younger boy excused himself to the restroom, Dylan scanned the thinning crowd and found Chester kneeling at the altar.

Squeezing his way past a few lingering members of the congregation, he knelt beside his new friend. Gently, he placed a hand on Chester's shoulder and began to pray that the longing in the older man's heart would be met with grace and compassion. That he would rest, satisfied with whatever ending came to him.

As the young man prayed, Chester wept.

He had assumed it was Dylan's hand on his left shoulder. But, midway through his prayer, when another hand was laid upon his right shoulder, he wasn't sure who had joined them. Two more hands were placed on his back before his prayer was finished. When he opened his eyes, he found Abby, along with her mother and brother, had joined them at the altar.

"Thank you," Chester said, wiping his tears on a handkerchief he kept in his back pocket. "I've been carrying quite the burden of late. Felt a tugging at my heart made me believe I should lay it down."

"There's always room at the cross for more," Angela said. "Is there anything we can do to help you, Mr. Wheatland?"

"Nothing I can think of Ms. Benson, but I sure appreciate your kindness."

"Abby said you and Dylan here got waylaid by some car trouble. Is there anything else troubling you?"

"Yes, ma'am. But there ain't nothing you sweet folks can do about it. Your prayers are all I can ask of you."

"You'll have them. Might I ask who's working on your car?"

"It's a truck," Dylan said. "We had it towed to a place called Junior's."

"They do good work," Angela said. "Kept our car running long past its prime. My husband and I know Junior. I'll call him in the morning and ask him to make you a priority. I can't promise anything, though. Junior's the best mechanic around here, so he stays pretty busy."

"Yes, ma'am," Chester said. "I was already working under the assumption I wouldn't make it to my destination on time. I've made my peace with it."

"Where were you boys headed?"

"Shreveport," Dylan offered. "Chester had a funeral to attend."

"Weird," Abby replied, looking to her mother.

"It is, indeed," Angela agreed.

"Momma was going to Shreveport," Shaun said, "but then daddy had to leave for a long haul on short notice, so momma didn't go."

"My husband, Ed, is a trucker," Angela explained. "He had a block of time off for the holidays but got called in for an emergency run. The money was too good to pass up, but it meant he had to leave early this morning."

"We opened all our presents last night," Shaun added.

"Now I see why Abby found it weird," Dylan said. "If we hadn't met you here, Mrs. Benson, we might have bumped into you in Shreveport."

"Especially considering Chester here was headed for a funeral, which was my reason for traveling, as well."

Chester's eyes narrowed.

"A funeral for who?"

"That's a long story," Angela said. "And a personal one."

Chester nodded.

"Tell her, Chester. Tell her where you were going," Dylan prompted.

Abby looked at Dylan with a question in her eyes. Dylan simply smiled at her and put his hand on Chester's shoulder.

"Tell them. We're all here at the altar with you. There's no judgment here."

"Over 40 years ago," Chester said, "I made the greatest mistake of my life. I wasn't a God-fearing man in those days. Was full of big dreams. Full of myself, truth be told. I was in love with a gal who was good to me, but I was planning to end things. I had me a job all lined up in California. Big money. Chance for a future. It never panned out but, at the time, it seemed like a once in a lifetime shot. There ain't no excuse for what I done. It's just the truth."

Chester's tears flowed freely, though his voice stayed calm and even.

"This gal, she came to me scared. I ain't had the chance to break things off yet or she'd likely have been downright terrified. She told me she was with child…my child. Said her parents would disown her for being with a black man. Said we had to run away."

"Did you?" Abby asked.

"All I could think in the moment was how it could be the end of everything I wanted. I couldn't take the job in California with a new wife and child in tow. Instead of seeing what a blessing it might prove to be, I only saw the potential for disaster.

So…I ran. Far and fast, straight to California and a job that wouldn't last. I left the gal who had been so good to me—a woman I truly loved as much as I was able back then—and I ran and never looked back. But it haunted me. It haunts me still. Some years later, I married my Delia. And I loved her more than I had ever dreamed it possible to love anyone. But I still remembered what a coward I had once been. I remembered my weakness and worried it was still in me. Feared I'd fail Delia the way I'd failed all them years before."

"Did you ever tell her?" Angela asked. "Your wife?"

"Eventually," Chester said with a nod. "I felt so much guilt. Especially since Delia and I weren't able to have any children. I'd thrown away my chance to be a father and likely ruined a good woman's life in the process. Whether my child was ever born or not, I don't even know. And it eats me up. Delia forgave me…as was her way. She saw who I wanted to be—who I was trying to be—and took it as fact. She was far better to me than I ever deserved."

"People change," Angela said. "Many men in a similar situation would never look back, Chester. They'd dodge and deny their guilt and it would harden their hearts. Sanctification is a work in progress, isn't it?"

"Yes, ma'am. And I've asked for God's forgiveness and know He's given it."

"Then what troubles you?"

"I ain't forgiven *myself*. Somewhere out in the wide world might be some boy or girl with my blood in their veins. It's their forgiveness I seek…seeing as how it's too late to get Loretta's."

Dylan saw the expression on Abby's face change and shook his head ever so slightly. She took the hint and remained quiet.

"This Loretta," Angela said. "I'm assuming you never saw her again."

"I looked for her over the last few years but didn't know what her married name had been. By the time I tracked her to Shreveport four days ago, she had passed. I thought, if I made it to her funeral, I might learn what became of our child. I know my cowardice might mean she was deserted by her family. It could be she got pressured into ending her pregnancy."

"Or she could've put it up for adoption," Angela offered.

"Possibly. I thought maybe there would be someone at the funeral who would know."

"Would knowing bring you peace?"

"At least I'd know. I ain't got much time left, you

see. Cancer got me and got me good. If there's a child out there who's mine, I'd like to know them. To at least ask for their forgiveness while I still have the breath to do it."

Angela placed a kind hand on the old man's face and smiled warmly.

"Would you do something for me, Chester? Would you humor a stranger for a moment?"

"Yes, ma'am. Your kindness earned you at least as much. You've made Dylan and I feel at home in a foreign land. It's God's work you've been doing."

"Have a seat," she said, pointing to an empty pew. "Abby, Shaun...would you two let Pastor Pitney know Chester and I need a few moments?"

"Yes, momma," both of Angela's children said in unison.

Chester and Angela took a seat in the pew. Dylan sat on the pew behind them. Angela studied the older man's eyes a moment before speaking.

"When I married my husband, Ed, I knew being married to a truck driver would be lonely sometimes. When the children came along, I had two little people to raise and love and laugh with. And Ed, when he's home, is the kind of Daddy I had when I was little. He loves these kids so unconditionally...is so ridiculously proud of them it always pains him a little when he has to go back on the road. We built a life here in this church and in this community. I see a lot of the same folks day in and day out, as you can imagine. A small town like this doesn't allow many secrets. Anonymity isn't really a thing we have much of. I say that to say I've never met a person who hasn't failed in one way or another. We all fall short of who we're meant to be, Chester. We all carry regrets. We all wish we could undo some of the things we've done."

Abby and Shaun returned and slid into the pew next to Dylan. Abby leaned over and whispered in Dylan's ear.

"Do you feel it?"

Dylan smiled and nodded.

"Growing up," Angela continued, "I was close to my folks. I didn't want for anything. Honestly, I was likely a little spoiled. They took me to church. Came to every softball game and basketball game. Gave me piano lessons even though I had no natural talent for the thing. But mostly they gave me the feeling that, no matter where I might go or what I might do and…even if they didn't understand it, they would love me. And no matter how grown I got, if I needed them, they'd come running. And they do. And they've been the same to their grandchildren."

Chester smiled sadly.

"They love you right," he said. "The way it ought to go."

"When I turned 21, my folks sat me down and told

me I wasn't their child by blood. I'd been adopted just a few weeks after I was born. They said I was the answer to a prayer they'd been praying for many a year. I'd be lying to say it wasn't a lot to process. As time passed, I realized it didn't really change anything. I still had my parents. I still had a blessed life. But one little piece I didn't know about…it nagged at me. A question still needed answering."

"You needed to know why," Chester said.

"Exactly. I didn't know where to start, so I let it go for a long, long time. I let my question linger and fester until just a few years ago. I had Abby get on the computer and dig around. I had to write letters and make a mess of phone calls to find out who my birth mother was. I had to dig long and hard to get her name. Once I had it, it took me another 6 months to work up the courage to write her a letter."

"Did she write you back?"

"She did. A long letter, too. And, next to her signature, there was a phone number. The first time I heard her voice, Chester, I wept. She did, too. Both of us just blubbering and sniffing and snotting. Took us 15 minutes to get any actual words out, I'd reckon. We talked for hours. I asked questions. She answered some. But she also asked me to come see her. I knew it would be awkward. So did she. She had been married for many years by that point and they had nearly grown kids. But I went, and they all welcomed me. We cried. We laughed. We told each other our stories. She asked me to forgive her, Chester, and for the life of me I couldn't understand what I should forgive her for. She'd done her level best in a tough situation. And, because she had, I had grown up with my Momma and Daddy loving me with all their hearts and raising me to be who I am. I can't even imagine who I'd be if my life had gone differently. I am who I am because of her choice. But sort of like you said earlier, she needed me to forgive her. So, I did."

"It's the very reason I was hoping to make it to Shreveport," Chester said. "To know the truth of things. To make amends…if that's even possible."

"And if there was a child out there," Angela said, "one you had never known, what would you say to them?"

The question broke Chester, though he'd considered her question often enough. He wept a moment before wiping his tears and nose on his handkerchief and attempting an answer.

"I'd say I was sorry and ashamed of being such a coward," he said. "And make it clear my running wasn't because of them or even because of their momma. It was only that I was selfish and lost. And if I had it to do all over again, I'd have supported the poor woman through her pregnancy. I'd have loved my child. My late wife Delia, rest her soul, would've loved them, too. Like the child was her own. It wouldn't fix nothin' to say those things, I know. But I'd hopefully set something free inside them… whatever pain or questions they might've been holding onto."

"And what would you hope for your child to say in return?"

"They wouldn't owe me no response, ma'am. Not after all I've done and *not* done."

"Still," Angela said, "in a perfect world, what would your child say to you?"

"That they forgive me…and that my foolish, selfish cowardice didn't wreck them too bad. I would hope they had a good life despite me."

Angela smiled at Chester, her own tears carving trails through her modest make-up.

"My birth mother's name," Angela said, "was Loretta Jones. Loretta *Madison* after she was married. She had been struggling with dementia for several years before my first letter. She remembered abstract things about my birth father. His smile. His nicknames for her. But not his name. She could never remember his name. And it made her sad for my sake."

"Loretta Jones?" Chester repeated.

"Yes, sir. Over the last few years, her health declined to the point where our calls and letters were infrequent, but I was glad I got to know her for what little time I did. I debated whether or not I should go to the funeral but, when Ed got called to take to the road, I decided against it."

"Are you saying—"

"I'm saying it's at least possible, Mr. Chester Wheatland, that you're my father. And, just in case you are, let me make something perfectly clear to you."

Chester's body trembled. His face was wet with tears.

"I forgive you," Angela said. "I forgave you long, long ago. But I'm glad I can say it to your face…because it's a good face. And there's no reason to carry such a burden around on your back because I had myself a fine family who loves me to this very day. Whoever you were back then, maybe I wouldn't have liked him very much. But you, sir, aren't the same man anymore. Time and God's good grace have changed you. Now, I'm gonna ask you to do something for me."

"Anything," Chester said. "Anything you ask."

"Then hug me, Chester. Because a hug from my father seems to me like a Christmas miracle. And I think it just might be one for both of us."

Chester hugged her tightly as she wept on his shoulder. Abby and Shaun wept, too, as did Dylan.

"Of all the places for my old truck to fall apart on

me," Chester said through his tears, "it brought me right to you. You were all I was hoping to find in Shreveport and here you were. Just waiting for me like a present under the tree."

The next morning, after a call to the mechanic to find out when Chester's truck would be repaired, he and Dylan walked back to Tucker's for breakfast where Angela, Abby, and Shaun waited for them in a large circular booth. They placed their breakfast orders before Abby asked:

"How long will it take to get confirmation you two are related?"

"Just a few days," Angela said. "I set up an appointment for Chester and I to get the blood samples taken this afternoon."

"Looks like I'll be here another day or two," Chester said. "Junior said I had a massive puncture in my oil pan, and he's got to order one from Little Rock. Depending on what time the part arrives tomorrow, he might not get to it until the next."

"You're welcome to stay with us," Angela offered.

"You and Dylan both."

"You're awfully kind," Chester said, "but I don't want to put you out."

"Well, I at least expect you both to come for dinner tonight."

"We wouldn't miss it."

Dylan kept his thoughts to himself, focusing instead on the people around him.

"I sure wished I'd have been able to apologize to Loretta before she passed," Chester said. "Though, from what you said, I'm not sure she'd have known me."

"I doubt it," Angela said. "I was glad to get to know her a little. I talked to her children just after she passed. She had gotten to the point where she couldn't even recognize them from time to time."

"It's a shame. I'm glad she made a good life for herself, though."

"From what I understand, she went to Oklahoma to stay with family until she gave birth. Had me in a hospital in Tulsa with the adoption details worked out in advance. Momma and Daddy took me home when I was just a few days old."

"I'm glad you were loved well," Chester said. "And I'm grateful to have found you. No matter what this blood test tells us."

Angela smiled.

"Ed will be back in a few days," she said. "I hope you get a chance to meet him."

"I'd like to…very much."

As they ate breakfast, everyone around the table told stories except for Dylan who remained largely quiet. As they exited the restaurant, Abby offered them a ride back to the motel, which they gratefully accepted. At the door to their room, however, Dylan paused.

"Hey, Chester?"

"Yes, son?"

"I think it's time for me to move on."

Chester looked back at the young man, squinting in the bright light of the morning sun.

"Move on?"

"I didn't really have a lot of time to work with," Dylan said, "but you've found the answers you were looking for, so I can go now."

"I'm not sure I follow."

"Sam had asked me to help you if I could. I wasn't sure how, at first. I was just along for the ride. But when we stopped for breakfast yesterday, I knew."

"Knew what?"

"That I needed to put a hole in your oil pan. Somehow I knew it would get us where we needed to be."

"You knew Angela was—"

"No. Although, once I met her, I suspected. Something about her resonated with me. No, I only knew my boss had a plan and it didn't involve us making it to Shreveport. I left some money on the table inside. It should cover your repairs. I didn't like deceiving you, I just hadn't known you long enough to be sure you'd trust me."

"Son, I'm not sure I'm following you."

"The point is, Chester, I think riding with you—knowing you—was as much for me as it was for you. You reminded me of some things I had forgotten. You've helped me realize I don't want to shy away from the things that frighten me. I have seen what awaits me. My good friend and mentor hopes I'll be able to avoid my fate, but I'm not sure I'm meant to. I trust the hands which guide me, Chester. I trust the Author of my story to work things out for my good. It may not go the way I imagine it, but He'll be there all the same. So, I'll trust Him and not shrink from what lies ahead."

Chester put a hand on Dylan's shoulder with concern in his eyes.

"What's all this talk, son? Where are you headed?"

"Home for now. To see my mom. To remember who I was before I started traveling. And then back to the good work of helping others."

"Am I gonna have to worry about you running off on your own?"

"No, sir. I'll be fine. Just promise me, whatever time is left on your account, you'll use it to love well and often."

Chester's eyes narrowed. With his right index finger, he pointed up toward the sky.

"Did He send you?"

Dylan smiled.

"Give Sam and Clay my best. And apologize to Angela and the others for me missing dinner. I have every reason to believe the blood work will prove what you and Angela already know in your hearts. Don't waste this time, Chester."

"I won't," Chester said, grabbing the young man in a bear hug. "Am I gonna see you again?"

"Probably not," Dylan said, tapping his chest above his heart. "But I'll keep you close. I've got too few friends, Chester. I'm honored to count you among them."

"The honor is all mine, son."

Dylan watched the old man reluctantly enter the motel room and close the door, then turned back to look out at the simple town and the nearby highway already busy with holiday travelers. It was the day after Christmas, and the hope born in Bethlehem so long ago was still alive and well in his heart.

Merry
Christmas!

A FREE GIFT

Scan the QR code or type the link below into the browser of your choice for a FREE story that reveals what Dylan Drake was up to after "Interlude" and before "The Road to Christmas."

"A Christmas Robbery" is available in multiple formats for your reading pleasure.

https://dl.bookfunnel.com/w79nwnhdan

Acknowledgements

Heidi, Shelby, Ember, and Jacob: Without your love and support, I couldn't do the work that I do.

Jason Webb, Ryan Jennings, and Scott Badley: You three have been my "ride or die" friends for so many years, I hardly remember life without you. I'm thankful every day for your continued presence in my life.

Chip Smitson, Chris Maddox, Mandy Schumacher, and Jason Henson: Moving across the country wasn't easy, but you have made the transition a pleasure with your kindness, generosity, and presence. Our friendship has lasted decades, and I'm forever grateful.

Hope Coffee Co.: The kindness and grace you offer each patron is as warm as the coffee you serve. I'm thankful for your presence in our little community.

J. Patrick Lemarr currently lives in Indiana with his wife, Heidi, and their children. When he isn't crafting horror and fantasy for Write Crowd Publishing, he is writing exclusive content for his Patreon supporters. The Lemarrs film reactions and reviews for movies and television on their YouTube channel, Pop Pop Fizzle, and discuss all things pop culture on their podcast, Pop Pop Culture.

To learn more, visit www.jpatricklemarr.com, where you will find links to social media, Patreon, and more.

You can also find him on
Goodreads at: www.goodreads.com/jpatricklemarr

WRITE CROWD PUBLISHING